Mahri-Jane Elliot was born in 1946 in South Norwood, London, is married, with three children, and lives in South Yorkshire and was the first female to work in a dubbing theatre in London.

Middlethorpe is dedicated to Miss Jane Austen, who left this world much too early, robbing it of all that she had yet to give.
Dec. 16th, 1775 – July 18th, 1817

Mahri-Jane Elliot

MIDDLETHORPE

AUSTIN MACAULEY PUBLISHERS™

LONDON • CAMBRIDGE • NEW YORK • SHARJAH

A CIP catalogue record for this title is available from the British Library.

ISBN 9781528908405 (Paperback)
ISBN 9781528908412 (Hardback)
ISBN 9781528960779 (ePub e-book)

www.austinmacauley.com

First Published (2019)
Austin Macauley Publishers Ltd
25 Canada Square
Canary Wharf
London
E14 5LQ

With thanks to my family for their help and support in this strange country of publishing.

My thanks also to Austin Macauley for the long-awaited opportunity to publish my work.

The countries of Upper and Lower Wittenstein are entirely fictional, as are their royal family. Also fictional are the place names of Hilling, Loosmore, Medford and Longburn, as is the Middlethorpe Estate that should not be confused with any of the same name.

The grammar of the time is, of course, rather different to that used today, so no complaints if you please. The dance known as Gathering into Sheaves is sadly also of my own fabrication but you are welcome to try it for yourself (entirely at your own risk of course).

Mahri-Jane Elliot.

Foreword

****

It is a truth universally acknowledged that Miss Jane Austen left this world far too early and took with her everything with which she might have endowed us if only she had been granted a few more years. I have so often heard the cry of anguish go up usually when the final episode of a dramatization of one of her divine imaginings has drawn to its close—if only there were more of them. Thus, those who love her are content to watch and to re-read the same six stories over and over, reaching a point in the process by which they know it all word for word but do they tire of them—of course not; would they have preferred more of them. Oh yes, indeed.

For a reason that eludes me, I have allowed myself to believe that I might be in possession of some ability to fill this aching gap in so many people's lives, having written three books in her style and using the English of the late eighteenth century and the Regency period but in a manner that I trust will appeal to the twenty-first century reader. By this, I mean that Jane Austen did not need to explain herself to her contemporaries, they already understood their own times but the further we leave her times behind, the more laboured the understanding of them becomes, which I believe is behind the refusal of many of today's readers, young and otherwise, to foster an appreciation of her work, perhaps on the grounds that Heathcliff is stuck somewhere on a Yorkshire moor waiting to be birthed through the pen canal and that rhetorical wit, however intelligently applied is no compensation. I have sought to address this in that at no time is the reader left in the dark as to what is going on and why it is of such moment to those of the day. In addition, I have included a glossary of the terms and cant used in this period and historic notes at the back of each book.

There was also that problem for Jane that she was quite unable to allude to matters deemed improper or never broached by a lady, which were considerable in number at the time, yet we may be sure that she was neither ignorant of these matters neither was she a prude. Of her private letters that her sister Cassandra did not dispose of, then lawfully, are not devoid of improper allusions or of hilarious, if spitefully rude quips about her family and neighbours; (she couldn't stand her mother and turned her into Mrs Bennet).

From sheer necessity, most people, including Jane Austen's family had a small holding which may have consisted of a pig or even two, a few chickens and ducks along with the kitchen garden and animals being both lusty and uninhibited about matters of procreation, especially if one had one of each kind, it was really not possible for those living on top of them to fail to understand the facts of life and could be most useful in eliminating the necessity of explaining such uncomfortable truths to the middling sort of girl. The poor, who invariably shared the one room, sometimes with the still living and breathing dinner, were never in any doubt of them and it was only the well-bred town girl, cut off from such vulgar knowledge and rich and aristocratic females who never saw the animals on their family estates except to see them graze the fields as they passed by in their carriages, that needed to be informed, usually the day before their wedding, what to expect and thus the habit of the vapours was born.

I, on the other hand, am not so constrained and like to hope that, with her blessing, I am acknowledging those things that she might have wished she could have delicately alluded to; for I assure all those who have not read an Austen biography that she was content to allude less delicately when the results were only passing through The Royal Mail and definitely not going to the printing press, which may have been the reason behind Cassandra's enthusiastic destruction of her letters which she must have begged the return of. But I also mention them delicately, for was I to do otherwise nothing I write would be in her image or the image of her times and that would deny the point of this project.

I am firmly of the opinion that Jane Austen's work satisfies a great need in those who are weary of the familiarity of the gutter which seems to pervade everything in our own times. From the minute by minute use of strident and colourful language by both sexes and all classes of society and the general behaviour which we find everywhere that courts no one's respect, along with the habitual practice of settling even the smallest disputes with the assistance of both verbal and physical violence, many are brought to wonder how we are come to this and how we can consider ourselves to be an improvement upon our forebears just because we wash more often and smell a little sweeter.

In an era when manners and proper speech determined who and what you were in the eyes of others, there is much for us to envy and a half-hearted yearning to return to those times to some degree affects many more today than one might imagine, though they would keep their yearnings secret whilst wilfully ignoring the inconvenient habit of hanging unfortunates for crimes that would today earn us six months at most at Her Majesty's pleasure along with a terrifying lack of anaesthetic. Despite these deficiencies and many others that would fall under the heading of mod con, the Regency era successfully pulls us in, in recognition of its unique position of having one foot in the old world and one in the modern, thus ensuring that all romantic antiquity remains intact but with the promise no one ends up burning at the stake anymore.

I have heard Austen disparaged as a writer of shallow matters and that she cannot be compared to the likes of the Brontës, George Elliot or Mrs Elizabeth Gaskell, to name but few of those equally disreputable females who had the nerve to put their imaginings and worse, their opinions on paper and make them public property—and in expectation of financial recompense to boot; the ultimate disgrace for a female, unless of course she was scrubbing floors or waiting on her betters. I beg to differ. She obeyed the writer's rule, to write only of what she knew. Lack of money and an abundance of constraint governed by her middling status in society did not permit her to know in any real detail how the disreputable lived, be they of the upper or lower orders and as for the passionate and expressive Brontës, the north was ever different from the south. I am long decided upon it that unforgiving meteorology (especially when it embraces vast amounts of bleak moorland) has dictated human behaviour down the centuries and the colder and the wetter the climes the more people are thrown together with predictable results, occasionally for the good but mostly ill. In this wise is society's immovable stand on manners overcome by human nature, being equally predictable.

The deaths of two sisters and their mother, eventually their brother Branwell and their maternal Aunt Elizabeth who had stepped into the breach, much hardship in a house so cold as to render it warmer out than in, a predilection for punishing, hand wringing religion along with an excess of artistic temperament, a debt-ridden junkie in their brother Branwell and all endured in a village (Howarth) which at that time, so I am given to believe, indescribably stunk to high heaven whatever the weather and was probably much behind the contents of the graveyard. I am not entirely against the notion that the Brontës were tinged with a hint of insanity and should judge each of these factors to be all that was needed to make even young ladies of the early Victorian parsonage improperly revelatory. Let us be reminded that, The Rev. Patrick Brontë threw the Ladies Magazines sent to his daughters into the fire because he objected most fulsomely to the love stories he discovered therein that no doubt were unremarkable and entirely escapist in content and perhaps to his way of thinking harmful, in that they encouraged the innocent female mind in hopes that would be unlikely to manifest in a filthy, disease-infested world, where the facts of life were very in one's face once the thin veil of maidenly innocence and modesty had been successfully breached. He was clearly doomed in the matter for his girls could be said to have taken their revenge most heartily. Perhaps they proved to narrow minded mid-Victorian society that when it came to what we now would describe as hormonal disturbance, females were actually capable of feeling what they had not experienced and since they did not inhabit the polite society of their grandparents or more southern climes the Brontë way was to be upfront about it. No wonder so many collars tightened.

Life greatly improved for them once their Aunt Elizabeth died and left them some much-needed funds and relative comfort after true hardship is a most releasing experience, especially to the artistic and expressive soul, whatever others might have to say about the spiritual value of the garret experience.

There you have it dear reader; my personal take on the Brontë style against that of Austen explained, if not creditably so on my part.

Jane Austen was also a daughter of the rectory but oh, the difference. Propriety clearly claimed more governance in Steventon and Chawton than the stormy northern wastelands of Yorkshire. Not for Jane a housemaid called Tabby to haul her through the beauties and horrors of untamed nature and the superstitions it engendered to sometimes terrifying levels of belief. She began her jottings merely to amuse her family on long TV-less evenings in a house that would have needed to count the vast cost of a book as delightful and exciting but probably not provident but as her hand became more confident she moved on to satirise the sensationalisms of the likes of Mrs Radcliffe. Austen was much too inclined to common sense and the rationalising of others melodramas, (the very antithesis of any Brontë). As youth departed and her disappointments, probably subconsciously designed on her part to free her pen from the tyranny of the womb and thereafter watching from the wings, she saw through the manipulations and machinations of others and through her writing counteracted them and all their works with some deliciously spiteful wit, often lost on the new reader for the lack of understanding that, in her time, when putting pen to paper one could be as rude as one pleased, even to royalty, just so long as one carried it out in a mannerly fashion that could even be mistaken for deference. Jane Austen may not have rung her own hands in sweaty passion upon a cyclonically enhanced moor but Marianne Dashwood most certainly did in Sense and Sensibility. In fact, she did it everywhere she could and quite graphically so. One has to feel it to write it.

It was also the height of the Napoleonic adventure in Austen's day and she has been regularly castigated for her lack of observance of it, over and above such scenes as the platoon of soldiers making their handsome presence felt in Pride and Prejudice; (cue, Mrs Bennet and her bosom heaving memories pre Mr Bennet.) Even Sir Winston Churchill remarked upon it; was he perhaps accusing her of not wishing to taint the callow scenery of the ball and the bower with the nasty and bloody business of war. It should therefore be considered that a relative by marriage to her Cousin Eliza, Count Francois Capo De

Feuillide was living in Jane's house one minute then suddenly and foolishly deciding upon the necessity of upping and leaving for France immediately, to check up on the condition of his estate at the hands of the mob, was hauled up on the scaffold and guillotined in a matter of days. It affected them all including Jane very deeply; Yes, Miss Austen knew about the nasty, bloody business of war and only consider in her defence: during the Second World War none hastened to the cinemas to watch war films, they did in fact watch some of the most escapist rubbish ever produced by the film industry, designed most purposefully to permit their audience to forget the horror of it, just for a couple of hours. What she did leave with us however, is a profoundly detailed record of the social history that so deeply and often cruelly affected her own kind and an equally sizzling record of the vastly intelligent humour and caustic wit in which they indulged against the enemy that today has been replaced by a coarseness that requires neither intellect nor unravelling to understand its meaning.

My first book, *Middlethorpe* (2014) may fairly be described as a novella being undertaken as a test case and a taster to see if I could do it and how it would be met.

It was written in the style of Lady Susan (1793-4), the story unfolding entirely through a series of family letters revealing a most wicked plot and the human capacity for such evil, even to one's own when the enemies of greed and ambition run mad. However, I have not forgotten humour for the demands heaped upon both sexes along with the expected manners of the day leave every opportunity wide open for it.

I offer my humble efforts as a 'homage, and a salute to one of the best of our literary giants who in her own time realised such small return for her mastery and was only permitted to sign her many hours of labour upon a little round table, 'by a lady', a lady indeed.

Author's Note
****

Throughout the centuries the survival of the 'great estate' not only depended upon the weather and the success of city investments but also the dowry that brides brought with them. The estates fed the nation, every county had at least one great estate and sometimes one or two modest ones also which were farmed entirely by the owner and without the presence of tenants but however they came none of us would be here now without them. But farming was always an ongoing learning curve and modern knowledge concerning crops only began to trickle in during the eighteenth century when the properties of chemicals which of course would have been from a natural source became better understood. The harvest festival of the church calendar was no romantic exercise, it was in truth a desperate 'thank you' to God for His decision to provide them with enough rain and enough sun and a surfeit of neither that allowed for a proper return on their hard labour, for drought was as feared as the deluge and a good harvest meant that seed had to be put aside against the year when either could ensure a famine in the land. As is the case today, while one part of the country enjoys perfect weather another labours under the grey skies that rot the grain or other arable crops. In a land as small as ours drought tends to be all encompassing and was feared greatly at a time when importing was not an option and a deal with another county with grain to spare would need to be brokered and all without modern communications. Not many people today realise how fortunate we are to be able to take our daily bread so very for granted and there are some who shamelessly take money for telling us how bad that bread is for us and the national waistline. Our forebears will be looking down in amazement at such a change in values.

Financial returns could be dangerously low on the occasion of a bad harvest and was a serious threat to the estate and that meant *all* the estate. House servants had to be paid, outside estate workers had to be paid, tenants needed to be looked after even if their crops had failed and their cottages maintained annually. Enter the bride with a healthy dowry. It was his lordship's duty to marry a good dowry; it was expected not only by his family but by his servants and tenants, she could be the difference between want and sufficient. Only God had the whip hand over 'plenty'. Love did not enter into the equation. If it should occur then the happy couple could think themselves extremely and unusually fortunate. As long as they could stand each other long enough and often enough to produce an heir and a spare against the death of the first, which was quite likely to happen then that was all that could be expected. But all was not unkind in the matter. Having produced the necessary 1st and 2nd heirs, her ladyship could feel free, provided she was entirely discreet, to find love. It was an unspoken gentlemen's agreement that any children of such an outside union would be brought up as one's own and therefore many an aristocratic by blow* bore the wrong name although one look at them was invariably enough to tell who had been with whom but woe betide anyone who was low enough to draw attention to it.

Thus were our estates successfully maintained and the nation fed, although some were better fed than others as remained the case right up until the Second World War.

During the eighteenth century many estates were put up as stakes at the gambling tables and lost in a moment. Servants and tenants alike must have dreaded being at the other end of a feckless lord but on the other hand they may have prayed that he would lose his estate to a better one. I have long been of the opinion that some lords along with untitled owners of large estates were not always so much feckless or indifferent to those who relied upon them but quite simply not up to it and did not have the strength of mind or abilities required to carry the onus of these estates and their many dependants. It needed an enormous sense of duty to all concerned and a mountain of business acumen to carry out. Just because one has inherited an estate doesn't follow that they are suited to the business. To the modern mind it would make more sense to sell them rather than lose them but in those times in doing so, a shameful loss of face would have followed and they would have been marked down as spineless, lacking a sense of duty, especially to one's family history and name and not the thing at all; but to drink to the point of amnesia (upon the following day) and wager the entire estate on the turn of a card was the lesser evil and happened, leaving everyone in a state of penury and the servants preying that the new owner would keep them on. Such a man would probably already have gambled away all other investments and the estate was all he had left to put up. Thankfully, the wonderful estates we still have in this country that are a source of as much pride to those who do not own them as those who do continue to be held by the same families who have always held them and continue in all duty to maintain them, albeit in a different way and for different reasons.

However, no matter how disgracefully her brothers may have behaved the daughter who could not be sold into marriage was an embarrassment to her family and herself. 'Old Maid' was the ultimate insult along with, ape leader and bluestocking, (see glossary). If her father was sufficiently wealthy he could leave enough for her to live on for life but it would have been unlikely to be a glossy lifestyle.

Daughters got a dowry with which to purchase a suitable husband. Second, third and subsequent sons got an education and an allowance until such time as they could make their own way in the world. The estate in its entirety would be inherited by the heir and no other; only in this way could the estate survive. A cup that is broken up into pieces is just that, a broken cup and can hold nothing. This practice was and still is known as primogeniture*; without it we would be a nation of broken cups.

Life was as precarious for the rich as it was for the rest. All were subject to its vagaries; Bonaparte, who could take out both the heir and the spare on the battlefield, meteorology, disease and those who tried to cure it. Whatever Mrs Bennett had to say on the matter of the common cold, (Pride and Prejudice—J.A.) it could be a killer at the time. A body already beset by vitamin and mineral deficiencies, although they might not have been hungry, draughty houses and germs spread by servants with poor personal hygiene and standards of washing up that would have been enough to kill the cattle, a cold could quickly become something more. No wonder poor Mr Woodhouse clung so desperately to the fireplace, even in mid-summer. (Emma—J.A.).

Since she could not earn her living the 'old maid' was required to earn her keep by being useful to the family and was often put upon almost as if she were being punished for her failure to snare a husband. If she were of the 'middling sort' she would have needed to become a governess if she had any education or a music teacher if not. Although usually coming from a good family the governess was looked down upon by every level of society. Regarded as neither fish nor fowl—neither servant nor family, though she lived alongside the family rather than the servants, the servants were often treated with more respect than she. This state of affairs remained right through to the end of the Victorian era, when it is possible that Jane Eyre by Charlotte Brontë finally brought the shame down where it truly belonged.

Many women caught in the spinster trap showed incredible strength of mind and courage in the face of the world's censure and survived in terrible poverty. That survival was much based on the old adage of necessity being the mother of invention. I believe that the women's movement was begun not by the few women with a voice but by these many 'old maids' albeit that they were unaware of it; that you did what you had to do even if it was frowned upon in order to buy bread. It is staggering to realise that in an era when most men doffed the cap to the lord and his lady that these same men who would have been regarded as the very lowest end of society would mock a lady from the upper end for her old maid status albeit not in her hearing, nevertheless she would have been aware of it.

It took profound courage for a genteel female in straightened circumstances to step out of 'her place' only to be rebuked by men with full stomachs and the right and the education to fill it again tomorrow and the day after. Thus God changes the world without our realising that it is happening.

Middlethorpe is a series of letters written by a woman, Athena Cranworth finding herself in such a situation. The letters are mostly one way in order that the dastardly plot that unfolds does so in the same manner as it would have been revealed to her—slowly. However I have not forgotten humour for there is plenty to be had when you find yourself at Middlethorpe.

****

The Ambassadorial Office Of
The Court Of St. James

To

His Britannic Majesty
King George III
Lower Wittenstein

****
****
***
*

To Mrs Katherine Cliffton
Cliffton Manor
Medford
West Suffolk

From the desk of
Ambassador's Chf. Sec
Edward Cranworth

July 7th, 1805

My dearest sister,

I write this in haste as I have already written to Mama and Papa to which I have included our sister Athena in the same missive. It has taken most of the time I have at my disposal this evening to plead my case to our parents for I am due at The Royal Palace of Lower Wittenstein shortly. This is no ordinary invitation for it comes directly from His Royal Highness Prince Friedriche. I have to tell you, Kate, that I have become engaged to The Princess Ursulinde of Lower Wittenstein and am this night to be presented officially to the nation at a grand ball given in mine and my betrothed's honour. I beg you, Kate, think this not ambition served above status but love rewarded. As you will no doubt have already gleaned from my tone, this is by no means a simple business and all is not entirely well with the prospect. Please believe me when I say that I am the happiest of men with my darling princess but in short I must relinquish my heirdom to the Kestlehurst Estate. As I have no brother this will cause the most dreadful sorrow and distress to my father but I am required to remain in this country at all times, I may not run one parallel with the other. Ursulinde is her father's only child and heir and unlike our own dear land, as a female she may not take the throne directly; we must produce a male heir and hope that it is born before her father's death. This would on the face of things appear an easy undertaking as my darling girl was just sixteen in early June but the prince grows a large swelling in his stomach which is kept secret from the people because a distant cousin of Upper Wittenstein, Rodolphe von Witten, an eighteen-year-old boy of much lower birth, in spite of his name who is of no consequence in his own country, harbours ambitions to take the throne of LW and no one will be able to stop it from happening. Worse than all this, the boy is detested and loathed even in his homeland. By all accounts he is a brute of the first water and it is said that if he ever finds himself in a position of power, even by default, he will bring the whole region to war and bloodshed, solely because he will own the power to do so and because he would enjoy it better than anything and thereafter by dint of civil war he would join the Upper and Lower Wittenstein's which neither wants for he would then become His Imperial Highness.

As you can see dearest sister, it is imperative that Ursulinde marry at the earliest possible time. Many have vied for her hand but she is an extreme delicate child and would have none of her suitors seeing them only as brutish fortune hunters little better than Rodolphe v W.

Sadly there is more. My darling girl's mother The Princess Metilde died giving birth to my beloved girl. She was born into this world in a state of pre-maturity and was herself not expected to live because of it. I am loath to tell you this and it is only because you are a married woman and a mother of five children that I feel able to do so; Ursulinde was cut from her dead mother's womb and underweight that it is a miracle she ever survived. There is of course the problem that a son may not be the first to arrive. As you know yourself, Kate, it took you four daughters before you were granted a boy and so it may be for Ursulinde and it has already become a great source of worry to me and the government of L. Wittenstein for time grows short.

The prince describes his own condition as being that of his grief for his lost princess wife growing ever larger by the day till it consume him but his physicians would have it otherwise and call it by another name. The poor lady suffered from a weak heart and my princess has unsurprisingly inherited the condition since she was born unfinished and even now is a small and fragile flower. I cannot but feel that early marriage and all its rigours will bode ill for her fragility but her father insists that her duty to the nation comes before all else and we, even in our comparatively modest inheritance of Kestlehurst must surely understand this position; an entire nation cannot be left to the tender mercies of the likes of cousin Rodolphe. She will have no other but me and would have me as soon as possible in order that others would cease their attempts upon her and leave her in peace to do that duty. I cannot but help think that it would have been better if his Royal Highness, her father had put as great a sense of duty upon his own shoulders and married again that he might have produced his own son but grief does much to make us hypocrites.

P.S.

Disaster has struck me in my great haste. The letter I wrote in fuller account to our parents was on my desk and at my elbow but I fear I must have knocked it into the waste basket. My man servant has been in while I have been writing, to attend to my fire which I have even at this time of year in the evenings for the summer here has been poor indeed and these vast buildings are most remarkable chill when the sun begins its slow descent. It is his habit to empty my waste basket into the grate to assist and I fear the letter has gone up in flames. I am vastly overworked at this time and I would beg you send this letter on to our parents when you have digested all its meaning to our family.

Your affectionate brother
Edward Cranworth

****

To Mrs Katherine Cliffton   Lower Wittenstein
Cliffton Manor
Medford
West Suffolk

July 8th, 1805

My dearest sister,

I write in far greater haste than I did just a few short hours ago, for events are running away with me and it would be no exaggeration to say that I am no longer the master of my own destiny but that must always be the case when one marries into a royal household.

I have not yet breakfasted and I must be back at the palace within the hour though I have had but two hours sleep; thus it has to be said that the ball was a resounding success and Ursulinde and I were accepted by all in such a manner as to make me believe that we shall be a most successful couple but and it is a huge 'but' the prince made it clear to me last night during a lull in the dancing that we must be married within the sennight*. His physicians have informed His Royal Highness that the swelling is now at the stage when [experience coming to bear] it is known that the time will soon be upon him when he will become so ill as to be unable to rule his kingdom and will be awash with Laudanum. Already the pains have begun in earnest whereas they were not beyond endurance but the present dosage is suddenly of only modest comfort to him. Therefore, my princess and I must be in place, she as the Blood Royal representing her father with me as her protector consort and a regnancy of court and government officials to govern in the prince's name or possibly suffer a usurpation by Rodolphe von Witten even before the prince has been permitted to breathe his last.

I am to be made a baron this very morning that I may stand beside my bride with some level of equality and all this hurry means that none of you my beloved family can be present at the wedding which is sure to derange our parents, particularly Mama. To have a son rise to such heights and not to be able to witness it must surely disappoint but the distance is too great to achieve in time.

My final request which I must make is that it is imperative Athena find a husband at the next Season. She is eight and twenty and Papa must surely be in high dudgeon over having to foot the necessary for yet another Season. If this one is as unsuccessful as all the others, I swear he will refuse her anymore; I go so far as to suggest that Papa up the dowry considerably even if it means selling something and peddle it about that she will soon be the sister-in-law of a reigning princess and a baron brother. It means that she will be stuck with a fortune hunter who is likely to leave her to get on with things while he stays in town for more decorative dalliances but even a brute is better than being an old maid. There are few months to go before the Season starts and she'll be all the nearer to nine and twenty. Athena is the eldest of us all and it is she must now produce an heir to take over the estate when the time comes as I now may not. I fear I must be plain with you and I do not expose you to language lightly but you are a female, Kate; tell her to drop her bluestocking* malarkey and to do something about her tendency to plainness. A man isn't going to agree to be leg-shackled* to a female who looks, sounds, thinks and behaves like one of his friends. It's decidedly rum*, Kate, rum indeed. I love Athena with a heart as full as any brother can but I must be as plain as she. She will end up the old tabby for sure if she's not more careful of the impressions she gives off and I know she don't want to be wearing the cap upon those chestnut tresses of hers for the truth of it is, she may not be pretty or winsome and the bloom may be wearing a bit thin now but she's a damned handsome woman but needs to be told so for I think she is inclined to a low opinion of her looks and compares herself ill to you, Kate, and thinks it a pointless exercise to even bother. Pretty her up and tell her to keep her mouth shut and to simper a bit; she won't like it but there it is.

I am sending this to you because Ma and Pa would not comprehend its full meaning not having received the first letter and you'll now have to send them both letters. It is all in your hands, sister. Will write to Athena myself as soon as all this business is over and settled and give her a bit of a pep talk and a shove in the back but right now I feel myself to be in the middle of a whirlwind at sea. Pray for me dearest sister for I am all in turmoil and quite exhausted already. By the by, congratulations on the birth of your first son, at last, Cyril I believe; très romantique. God's speed to the next one 'old girl', Cliffton must have a spare you know.

Your affectionate brother
Edward Cranworth.

****

To Mrs Katherine Cliffton   Miss Athena Cranworth
Cliffton Manor   Kestlehurst House
Medford   Hilling
West Suffolk   East Suffolk

August 10th, 1805

Dearest Sister,

I am all grief now that you have gone home to your husband. It was more than all the world to me to see you and the girls; how they have grown. We were all surprise to have your letter warning us of your imminence, so much so that Mrs Burridge, who is normally of a most obliging nature, was heard saying to Quigley only yesterday and in the huffiest of tones that she hoped next time she would receive more than two days' notice of your intentions, on account of the size of your entourage. I only tell you all this now on account of the little I saw of you alone when you were here. But for my part it was divine to be able to meet my new nephew while still so fresh to the world, for it was not so with the girls, each of them was much grown before we caught first sight of them. Baby Cyril is a delight if only for being a boy. At only two months of age you must own dear Kate that he forced his opinions upon us all day and night, it is, therefore, no surprise to me that Mr Cliffton made no objection to your coming to stay with us so soon after your confinement although I must own to some reservations concerning the shaking all about in the carriage of your still fragile body and the baby who must have found the experience a most colicky one. Cordelia at five years is a most decided and determined young miss and must be said to take after you in this matter. I cannot be asked to see anything of Mr Cliffton in her and this makes me wonder at the vagaries of nature. Of course, at just four dear little Georgina copies her big sister in everything and thus is their nurse driven to despair. Three-year-old Alice makes up for the pair of them by being so good as to have had us wondering if she had gone home on her own. Only little Fanny at a mere two years old could be relied upon to be of small concern and was as content as any child I ever saw to build with bricks and knock them down again. Perhaps she mistook the pastime for having control over her world, I pray she beguiles herself in this belief for as long as possible for the truth will come in all its unhappy condition soon enough.

It is at this point in my deliberations over your unexpected visit that I admit to being most concerned on your behalf dearest Kate. Forgive me if you think that in spite of my seniority I should not speak to you thus, being unmarried but I feel myself unable not to. You must own that having five children by the age of two and twenty is, whilst not unusual, especially amongst our tenants, well, shall we just say it is enough for any married woman. I am sensitive to your husband's need for a son and heir and that this is possibly why you have been required to continue on the road of maternity but we are all too, too aware of how fragile children's lives are [have not our own parents lost two boys between mine and Edward's births, one to the morbid throat* and another to measles] and that for this reason, Cliffton is unlikely to be content until he has another son to ensure an heir. It is true that you have proved yourself a strong, young woman whose ability to bear young without the horrors attendant upon lesser mortals but I could wish with all my heart beloved sister that you be allowed a rest for I would not lose you if my heart is to remain unbroken.

I should have liked more of your society while you were with us for I kept losing you and Mama and Papa amid the gardens but I shall not complain for it allowed me to forge affectionate bonds with my nieces who are likely in the future to have more to do with this aunt than most on account of her maidenly condition. Now, dearest Kate, you are gone to your own home as suddenly as you came to ours and I am all loss and I also miss Edward so much and bitterly resent that I could not share his birthday a month since; at four and twenty he probably thinks himself middle-aged. I do hope he will be allowed home soon but he has not written for an aeon.

What ill news has just been brought to me in the last minute by Mama's lady's maid, for she tells me that tidings have just arrived concerning that of my own maid Gracie. It would seem that her mother has become most ill and her father has need of her at home. This has come as a great blow to me; as much as I suffer for Gracie in this matter, I wonder if she will be able to return to me.

God bless you and keep you beloved sister and remember me fondly to Mr Cliffton for I am really very fond of him also.

Your affectionate sister,
Athena Cranworth.

****

To Cliffton House

Kestlehurst House
Hilling
East Suffolk

August 14th, 1805

Dearest Kate,

I am the most wretched and miserable of creatures that ever had need to put pen to paper for my life is at an end. Think not this statement an overdramatic one for it is the truth. Last night Papa called me to his study whereupon he informed me that he would not be affording me another Season. I quite expected this Season to be my last for by anyone's reckoning it seems an ill use of so much money to be spent on any woman beyond the age of eight and twenty. Has it not been a source of shame to me that Papa should have spent so many thousands of pounds upon me since my come out with no satisfactory outcome?

Papa railed against me for my bookishness and was cruel enough to say that I could no longer be described as a bookish miss but must now forever be tagged a bookish old tabby and to henceforth go and cover my plain and uninteresting hair with the cap and to make as much display of my blue stockings as will impress whatever company I happen to be in, for it was certain that they should never be suitors. He went on to say that my clothes were as unfashionable as that of a governess and that no one knew if I had any sort of décolletage since no one had ever seen it, which we both know to be quite untrue but Papa was in such a 'flight to the boughs'* that I was too afraid to speak in my own defence.

At this point in our one-sided conversation, our father rose out from behind his desk and paced the room as if he were waiting the start of battle and I stood head bowed in shamed silence, whereupon he renewed his attack upon me, this time for my conversation at table where any hoped for suitor were present saying that mine was more suited to the gentleman's club and that he wouldn't be surprised if I were to henceforth speak in the worst of tavern cant because he was well aware of my use of it in private although I would never bring shame upon myself or my family by using it in company. This he knew to be the most unearned of insults and he had the grace to blush at it, but oh, Kate, it was as if he had been got up to this, for surely if these things had been on his mind for so long or if even half true he should have spoken of them before now. What is my life to be hereon in? As you know there are few opportunities for any kind of social life in Hilling and the chances of meeting anyone suitable are thin indeed. Therefore, I must settle myself to the future as a spinster and maiden aunt. Papa has said that he would rather put what would have been uselessly spent on the next Season into investment to keep me for when he and Mama are no longer. The best I can hope for is that Edward will be generous enough to allow me to see out my days at Kestlehurst hopefully making myself useful to him for he must have children of his own. I cannot help but feel that if I could appeal to our brother he would take my part in the matter and encourage Papa to invest in my hopes one more time but I am told I may not write to Edward on any matter for there is a deal of trouble in Lower Wittenstein and though I am assured he is not in any personal danger he is much distracted and burdened by the situation and must not be bothered with trivial domestic matters and anyway writing would be a waste of time as by all accounts the mail is not getting through which seems a dire situation for the diplomatic service. Dearest Kate, you have gone from us just when I needed you the most and I feel isolated from all wise council. Men may be as free as they wish from the tyranny of marriage but a woman who finds herself thus situated is not free but incarcerated in all things including that of financial stricture and an object of public ridicule. Can this really be considered a trivial domestic matter?

There is a terrible pain where my heart once lived; my appetite has quite simply disappeared and I have not slept. I beg you write me quickly for I have need of your mind on this most miserable of deprivations to which I have taken very ill.

Your loving sister,
Athena Cranworth.

****

To Cliffton House

August 17th, 1805

My most beloved Sister,

I was grateful to receive your early response to my news and your sisterly commiserations but I have to tell you, things have changed in a manner I could never have foreseen.

I am to become companion to our Great Aunt Middlethorpe who I know to be six and eighty years of age so it might as well be nurse companion for how else could it be at such advanced years? I am to be buried alive and you know as well as I, Sister, the famous longevity of the Middlethorpes I have heard it oft said as you must have also that if a Middlethorpe reaches their three score and ten in good health, one can safely assume another twenty years if not a little more. As we are all Middlethorpes through Mama, I can only hope for my part that I never reach my seventieth birthday at all for to endure such a career as has been fashioned for me by my own family is not to be borne but naturally dearest Kate I wish for you as I do Edward the longest and happiest lives possible.

On the 14th just past, I saw Maudent, the lower footman, coming out of Papa's study carrying a letter which he was, I have since learned under instruction to take to the mail office but Maudent cannot read or write and therefore would not be able to tell who the letter was for. I cannot help but think that this was a deliberate act of Papa's so that I should not know what was about to happen to me for our letters are always collected by the mail boy who comes out twice a day and I should have seen it lying on the salver. Today a letter came for Papa and Mama the writing of which I did not recognise. It is safe to assume that this was from Great Aunt Middlethorpe agreeing to a request from our father to get me off their hands and keep me out of the way of embarrassment to them for it is certain that a daughter they cannot sell is just that.

So there it is, Kate. I am bid start my packing immediately and to take all that I possess. From this, I may deduce that our parents do not expect to see me for a considerable length of time. No woman was more punished for the sin of failing to secure a husband than I for I am told that whether her mother die or recover, Gracie must remain to take on her mother's duties for the time being and, therefore, I am not to have my lady's maid and I must imagine she can only bewail bitterly over it for she is not inclined to the life of the farm and much preferred to be with me in a more genteel situation. I taught her all she knows, she can read and write as well as you or I, though her vocabulary is limited to her station and can do simple mathematics for domestic purposes, indeed the other servants rely on her to help them when they are confronted by something that is beyond their own abilities. I do not understand why I may not keep her for if I am not there, she may not return to Kestlehurst. I think I shall insist that I shall not go without her even if she must follow on later.

I am to leave for Middlethorpe, it is also the name of our great aunt's house and estate, in just a few days' time. Papa has gone himself this very morning to arrange the transport and I am to have a coach to myself, for there will be no room for other passengers with so much luggage. My past and my future will be packed in it but I declare, my misery will take up most of the space. I am to take Maudent with me who will be required to guard my possessions during the night by sleeping in the stables with the coach while I must brave the coaching inn alone and unchaperoned for want of my lady's maid. Perhaps Papa thinks that I am so very plain as to be entirely without need of a chaperone. I have never felt more like a stranger to my own family and in my own home than I do at this time. What has happened, Kate? I appeal to you, will you not speak for me to our parents and tell them that what they are doing to me is too cruel and the outside of unjust; they must surely listen to you having command of respect owed to you as a married woman and mother of children. I own that I am inclined to be opinionated on account of my learning, by which I mean reading for I have had no teacher to take me beyond what has been considered suitable for a female and I can only accept that I am to blame in this which leaves our father with the unfortunate matter of putting aside sufficient funds to keep me for the rest of my life and I have been forced to consider the possibility that he has had to ask Great Aunt Middlethorpe to share this burden because he is not as financially sound as we might have assumed him to be, or perhaps he has lost money on The London Stock Exchange [though I know not how one could lose with India bonds* or 'Consuls']* but to blame me for my plainness is I think, unfair. I may be held responsible for my appearance but not my looks and a little feeling on their part for my own might have been a kindness one could expect from one's nearest flesh and blood.

But not for this your unloved and rejected sister the felicity of familial support. I am to be cast out into full view of a world that already knows of my failure. When I say full view, what I mean is that my absence from society and any further 'Seasons' will be statement enough of my condition henceforth and the false sympathies of an equally false sisterhood will be heard echoing around every ball and rout, until finally they all forget my name and it will be as if this 'old maid' were never born though our father will have it, he will never be allowed to forget such a begetting, in that he must be obliged to keep starvation from my door till I breathe my last. Oh, what an unprofitable daughter.

I am your wretched but ever affectionate sister,
Athena Cranworth.

****

To Cliffton House

The Three Bells Inn
Blessingham

August 21st, 1805

My dearest Kate,

At last I am able to write to you for I certainly think that I will not be writing to Mama and Papa ever again and the further I get from that place that was once my home, the more keenly I feel their rejection and the continued deprivation of my maid Gracie only serves to make it all the worse. You will surely own that one's lady's maid is also one's friend as well as servant and more than that, we quickly become their friend for we are so very much together [strangely so, more than family] and have I not been her servant when she has been ill for it is I who knows best her needs. Do not you find all this to be so with your own lady's maid? I should like to know your mind on this matter.

Let me begin the tale of this journey by telling you that my spirits have lifted sufficiently for me to have felt the first pangs of an adventure. In spite of the great weight that the coach is carrying we have hurtled through the countryside at an alarming rate for I am told that the journey is just two days, if there are no delays and that all effort should be made in the maintaining of this timetable if we are to keep to the arrangements that have been put in place for me and my safe conduct. Females who find themselves in coaching houses they do not know the fitness of because the journey has overrun can also find themselves in a deal of danger or a level of un-cleanliness that takes its revenge upon one's stomach anon which is the worst of fates to befall when one is in a coach but at least I have Maudent who is beside himself with excitement.

Having never left Hilling in all his twenty years except to go into town on errands he is hanging out of the coach window at all times and waving at everything living and inanimate alike. Being required by Papa to sleep in the coach house is as nothing to him while the coachmen take rooms over it and sleep in comfort. I have seen little of the inn, The Three Bells, for being unchaperoned, I must take my meals in my room and have been required to order for Maudent. The food was acceptable but not desirable. Later this evening I myself will take him out a single mug of porter, for the rest he will have to take coffee or chocolate, I cannot have him in his altitudes* whilst in charge of all my worldly goods. For this reason, I shall keep him company awhile, whatever anyone thinks about it. Thieves are cunning creatures and would take advantage of a green footman and offer him drink. By morning he would wake to find us robbed and I swear Papa would have him hanged or at the very least deported.

As the days are still long I have been able to take a look at the surrounding area. It is all farmland and there is nothing here just this inn, a duck pond and three churches at equal distance from us by which I gather the place comes by its name and the hostelry likewise. My bones are quite rattled by the journey and wonder what condition I shall be in when we reach Middlethorpe. I had to pay the coachmen a little extra to watch my possessions that Maudent might accompany me on the walk and he made so bold as to take my arm as my back was aching dreadfully from the journey and my limbs responded with an unwillingness to support me in the usual manner. He was quite the gentleman and I think that he will make a good and gentle husband for one of the Kestlehurst maids.

A maid has just entered my room to take our orders for breakfast and has agreed to hand this letter into the post in the morning for which I shall give her a little money for herself. It seems she has also been assigned to me as a lady's maid at bedtime.

Perhaps I am better taken care of than I thought but I would much rather I had Gracie.

Your affectionate sister,
Athena Cranworth.

6.30A.M.

P.S. I have broken the seal on my letter that I might tell you that it was five am when I was thrown all about in my bed by the incessant ringing of the bells of the three churches, all at once. I collect they remove the farming community from their beds and likewise the inn's servants. The ducks responded by much fearsome squawking and quacking whilst shooting up and down the pond, which performance I imagine they undertake every morning. I otherwise slept well although I suspected that I could smell the previous occupant of my room upon the bed linen.

****

To Cliffton House

Middlethorpe
Loosmore
Hampshire

August 23rd, 1805

Dearest Sister,

As you see we are safely come into Hampshire and much
relieved for our journey went ill with us yesterday that we
thought it should take the extra half day and we would have to
put up at The Crown at Oakham Wells. The rain was so heavy as
to make the roads impassable in some places and our progress
was much impeded by it. Our wheels became trapped in the mud
and the horses made themselves clear on the matter, thus were
we obliged to find a spot to wait up. The rains did indeed cease
eventually and the sun which followed was so fierce as to dry up
the flash floods far more quickly than we could have hoped
allowing us to continue albeit slowly, thus we were behind time
and the horses exhausted by their efforts. The Crown was full by
the time of our arrival and no rooms were to be had on account
of other travellers having had the same trouble as we, which
though very worrying at the time I was also relieved for I thought
it a dubious sort of establishment that otherwise would not have
found itself on the list of the officially sanctioned and Maudent
who has been so protective of me and my welfare said that we
should not stay anyway even if there were rooms to be had and
that we should just change the horses and drive through the night
if it comes to it, which is what we did.

Dear Kate, I never was so frightened in all my life. The
natural world of the countryside is a delight to the soul in the
daytime but once night is fallen, particularly on long, unknown
highways and turnpikes lined with dark, menacing trees, it is the
most terrifying place to find one's self and most especially when
there is no moon. I pride myself on not being a silly or fanciful
woman but it is well-documented that the days of the
highwayman are not yet entirely gone and the hiding places are
so many, from one end of a road to the other in truth. Thank
heavens all the gibbets en route were unoccupied for I cannot
bear to see it. Maudent held my hand all the way reassuring me

every inch of the journey that he would not allow anything unspeakable to happen to me and that he would die before my honour became the subject of interest to the unworthy. Oh dear Kate, I do believe that Maudent has formed a most unfortunate tendre for me yet he has been with us since he was twelve years of age and barely acknowledged my existence before now. It would seem that unusual situations can make one suddenly attractive, or perhaps it is the case that another side to one's character becomes visible. It is somewhat vexatious to learn that at eight and twenty one can attract the devotions of a puppy, however unsuitable but a healthy dowry cannot provoke any such; I am all confusion. Do you think that the lower orders are not so put off by plainness or the frankly unbeautiful on account of their own condition, usually being in such want as they are all subject to the problem, as beauty rarely flourishes in deprivation?

When we, at last, arrived at Middlethorpe, it was eleven o'clock at night and thus were we saved from having to travel all night and were greeted with a mixture of relief and uproar for we were expected by four in the afternoon so I suppose that it did take the extra half day. Our great aunt had had a search party out all evening but when we arrived all were in bed save for an elderly servant who had been left to sleep in the kitchens against our finally making it through. I fear much noise was made by the bringing in of my trunks and boxes enough to wake the entire household save for our great aunt who remained resolutely abed and I thought this a clear indication of her condition. The elderly manservant whose name is Twigg took Maudent and the coachmen off to the kitchens for the food that had been left for them. Maudent was given a truckle bed in the pantry for the night and the coachmen went to the stable block. Once all my possessions were safely conveyed into the hall and the doors locked and bolted, the servants who had been in attendance in their nightshifts suddenly all disappeared back to their beds and in silence I was conducted by Twigg, who like his name, was far too bent and feeble to carry my night bag up the grandest staircase I have ever seen albeit by a single candle flame and shown my room where a jug of still warm washing water and a tray of food had been left for me. Twigg lit my bedchamber candle from his own and bid me goodnight. I ate my supper and I put myself to bed whereupon I fully intended to weep myself to sleep but I was much too tired to do so and just fell asleep instead.

I was awoken this morning at the late hour of nine o'clock by the maid who brought my hot chocolate. Fully expecting to find myself in the most oppressive house I was delighted when she drew aside the curtains and to see that I was in quite the most cheerful of bedchambers a young woman could wish for, even one just two years off official middle age. The maid introduced herself as Mary and said that she was two and twenty and was to become my lady's maid. At first, I resented the fact that she was not Gracie but immediately corrected myself. It is not the girl's fault that she has been wished upon an ungrateful wretch who would much rather the one whom she had trained up and had become a friend and yes, even a confidante. Now that the journey is over and I have time to think I wonder that Gracie could not bear to say goodbye after twelve years in my service. I suppose I must accept it as a compliment and indication of her feelings for her mistress that she made herself so scarce even before my departure let alone her own which in the end came first. Is it not a peculiar fate that the tenures of mine and Gracie's living at Kestlehurst both came to an end at the same time?

As I have been left to sleep in this morning I am to have my breakfast sent up and at this very moment, a bath is being prepared in my room. Servants are coming in and out with pails of hot water and I am more grateful than I could have thought possible for I am extremely dirty. The mud that clung so decidedly to my dress and stockings has passed through both and my legs look like those of an urchin child, moreover, I carry the smell of linen used before me and probably more than once and I would have Papa know that for future reference The Three Bells should be struck from the 'recommended list'.

I must now quit this letter for I must be bathed and dressed so that I may go and sign Maudent off duty. Papa has given me a purse of money for him to get him back to Kestlehurst in reasonable if modest comfort to which I shall add my own. It will leave me short for the rest of the year but I have seen that his need is far greater than mine. I have also written a letter for him to present to Papa with my personal commendation of his conduct and fine sense of duty and that he should, in due course, be considered for first footman for if left to Papa, he will leave

Maudent an under footman forever. I now wish that I had known John Maudent better for I would not have him ignorant. I fancy I see a primitive nobility of intent lurking in his unworldly youth and would have it exploited to good cause.

From one of my boxes in the hall and I know exactly which one, I will retrieve a book of letters and one of numbers which I used to teach Gracie and give them to Maudent in the hope that I may teach him by corresponding with him. How very novel a plan, do you not think it, Katy dear. It will give me something to live for and serve to keep my mind off my own condition. I will write again as soon as I have got the measure of how things are here at Middlethorpe; by that I suppose what I really mean is, as soon as I have met our great aunt and am fully appraised of the nature of the misery that lay before me.

Pray for me, Kate, for we are not raised in the manner of servants and I cannot fail more or be lost forever.

Your loving sister,
Athena Cranworth.

****

To Cliffton House

August 25th, 1805

Darling Kate,

I hardly know where to begin. My first morning was much taken up with the transportation by a number of servants of my boxes and trunks from the hall to my bedchamber, thereafter emptying them and putting everything away. Mary was quite dizzy and exhausted when we had finally finished. Strangely, the completion of this task was not accompanied by the despair that I had expected to overtake me, indeed there was a deal of levity and in the end, elation but from what cause I cannot tell. When all was done I went downstairs for luncheon during which occasion, so I was informed by our ancient relative's secretary, an utter fright by the name of Mr Quentin Pomphrey, [equally ancient and determinedly old-fashioned in his appearance] that I was due to meet our great aunt for the first time. I was much of the mind that she probably did not come down until luncheon most days and retired early. I have always understood that sleep is a major requirement amongst the aged and that it comes upon them at odd times all through the day. Imagine my astonishment when the lady herself appeared in the dining room in such manner as I thought that I was not the only guest in the house. I confess that I had looked for evidence of a wheeled chair on the ground floor so that she might be taken around her grounds for I considered it unlikely that she would be able to walk much, if at all. And now I could see why I had not found such evidence for standing before me was a straight-backed lady, of some fashion I might add, who arrived before me without even the aid of a walking stick. I made my curtsey and introduced myself and waited to be told that this was surely not my great aunt. The lady kissed me on my right cheek and announced, "I am your Great Aunt Horatia Middlethorpe, child, and I welcome you to this house. I trust that we will bide very happily together."

I confess that I took in all I saw of her with what must have appeared to be some degree of rudeness on my part but in my defence, I think she must be used to it, for unlike her secretary she had adopted the modern fashion without allowance for years, but yet with dignity for she hid her ageing décolletages with muslin and lace. She wore a cap that did nothing to hide her hair but was the merest bow to the demands of society upon the older woman, being so small as to reveal most of hair which is not even now entirely grey but still boasts a hint of the once coppery chestnut colour of her best days. But Kate, our great aunt wears cosmetics, [as does her secretary]. I declare there was corn flour on her face, soot upon her eyelashes and a subtle hint of rouge on her lips and cheeks. I cannot but say she looked most handsome and would turn the heads at any gathering but for all the right reasons, [unlike her secretary]. All this I took in at a glance but I fear my amazement was obvious and had I been more ladylike I should have hid it better for she said to me: "Do I come as a surprise to you, child? Did you suppose me to be in my dotage, that you should be reading books and newssheets to me while I listened best I could through a trumpet? Perhaps you had visions of rubbing oil of lavender into blackened skin whilst avoiding my bad breath caused by the rotting of teeth."

I thought I should weep for shame for I had expected all these things—or much like but she generously erupted into gales of laughter and said, "I am a Middlethorpe child, as are you and we die in good order, those of us who reach beyond our seventieth year as if we were still forty, that is. Though not all of them are as blessed; had you known your Great Uncle James, my husband and my first cousin, you would have seen that for yourself. Now, he was a poor specimen. He caught a cold and died in a great state of fever in our first year of marriage and didn't even live to see his first born son which was as well for he was stillborn— and worse. Thus, here I am in this great house, still alone and caring for my husband's estate for as long as God wills it." I thought I saw that she still carried the great sadness about her and I am most suddenly resolved to be as good a companion to our great aunt as I can be. What do you suppose she meant by— 'and worse'?

After luncheon which is a very modern thing, do not you think and was very light and much consisted of fish and vegetables followed by fruit. Just think, Papa would be scandalised by such fare but I found it acceptable and sufficient as Aunt keeps country hours and dinner is taken at five pm rather than midday.

I have been conducted on a tour of the house and it is extremely grand, boasting a ballroom of such size and proportion the whole world could dance in it and a library that makes the one at Kestlehurst look rather modest both in size and it must be said content, which as you can imagine thrills me to the core of my most unfeminine being and will satisfy my insatiable need for knowledge until I am no more. I have walked endless walls of portraits and landscapes, day rooms, evening rooms and rooms devoted to every necessity of business and pastime and all was light and cheerful although very grand and imposing. There was not a dark corner anywhere and one must applaud the leaving behind of the Elizabethan and Jacobean styles for I fancy they always look haunted even if they are not so. Middlethorpe's chandeliers are enormous and carry so many candles I wonder that any chandler could cater for them all in the course of a year, although, of course, they are not all lit at the same time or all the time for I do not think that this place has been bought with profligacy nor known for vulgar show.

I was then taken below stairs to meet the servants in their own quarters—I have to say I found this quite the most novel approach but I could not but observe that none of them panicked or scuttled about at Great Aunt Middlethorpe's incursion. Should Mama or Papa have ever ventured below the ground floor, I warrant our servants would have broken out in nervous hives. Tomorrow I am to be taken around the grounds and to meet the gardeners. From what I can see from the windows, there is much to be taken in and fancy I shall be out there from dawn till dusk just counting the flower beds and that is before I even reach the walled kitchen gardens and greenhouses where I am told they boast fireplaces and things grown out of season. Oh Kate, everything here is so vast and vastly novel.

I pray that Maudent is almost arrived safely and not been robbed on the road or in a tavern for as much as he looked after me, I also looked after him. Young men of all classes are so much inclined to take up the tankard and having done so cannot find the strength of mind to put it down again and are thereafter the victims of those who either refrained or are better trained in the business of holding their ale. I suppose I cannot hope that Papa will write and put my mind at rest but I do hope I can expect a letter from you soon, Kate, for I am desperate for every little piece of news. If there is any chance of communication to or from Edward please, please have Papa tell him where I am, send him my address for I know not if he has any memory of Middlethorpe, I am sure he will want to know how I do in my new life. My dearest, love to you all as always.

Your affectionate sister
Athena Cranworth

****

To Cliffton House

August 30th, 1805

My Dearest Kate

I cannot understand why you have not yet written, the weather has been all that one could expect of August and the roads dry and therefore, the mail has been getting through, for Great AM has been receiving letters of business from London each day; I can then only think that you must be ill. I have been quite worried that this would come about with so many children to your merit but baby Cyril is yet so young that [if I can put it delicately] one might assume your constitution may not be replenished for some time to come and I pray that the 'little spare' may not yet be on his way. Please have a care Kate, I beg of you. I will, therefore, wait as patiently as I am able for your next letter. I am pleased and relieved to say I have received a somewhat brief missive from Mama assuring me of John Maudent's safe return and my note of commendation was read with some surprise and even amusement and judging by Mama's curt wording even some annoyance at what she supposes to be my impertinence which I thought to be a strange reaction but then all telling have become strange to me recently which concern my family.

It would seem that, as I am to remain at Middlethorpe for some time, my great aunt would have me well-equipped with the knowledge of how Middlethorpe is run. A barouche was rigged for us yesterday and I was taken to all of Aunt's tenants one after the other and all without her secretary. Much mileage had to be covered and for this reason, Aunt does not stay more than fifteen minutes with each unless necessary; enough time to enquire after their health and that of their children and any discontent and to establish the condition of their cottage, for winter will be upon us soon and all repairs must be made before the autumn rains make any problems worse. Great Aunt is most assiduous in her care for her tenants and is quite genuine in her sensibilities for their good comfort and welfare. How I wish that Papa and Mama were the same. Papa has always maintained that farmers have nothing to do through the winter months but to mend their fences but I fear this is not so. I cannot forget that the Tullber family died of the fever in the winter of 98 for want of the re-thatching of the holes in their cottage roof which Mr Tullber was no longer sufficiently agile to mend and having no son. Papa insisted that he had supplied the materials and that it was up to Tullber to do the work. Therefore, my mind is much at ease in the case of the Middlethorpe tenants and it would seem that they are of the same mind for they were most glad to see us and made much fuss and ado of me and all without exception pressed us to refreshments which you can imagine bore its problems.

Great Aunt required me to make notes in a special book which she keeps to the purpose of all the tasks and considerations that must be attended to for each tenant. I suggested that she ought to have had her secretary to help her on these rounds. To this, she replied that any man who dressed like a mid-eighteenth century ladies boudoir had no place anywhere near a farm and caused far too much mirth amongst the tenants especially as he drops wig powder everywhere he goes and sets off the farm dogs with his painted face. She preferred he keep to the many other affairs of the estate and leave her tenants to her as it was quite pointless for him to interfere knowing she would only get annoyed with him for his chilly efficiency, by which I think she might mean parsimony [which hardly seems to match with his courtish appearance] and do things her way in the end that he might as well concentrate on making money for her from her investments, just in case there is ever a bad year for she says, she is unable to offer herself on the marriage market as a dowry the size of England wouldn't buy a rich handsome husband at her age. At this, she roared with laughter in such a manner that I felt compelled to join her though I am definitely relieved that we were on our own at the time, apart from the coachman who is well used to everything apparently. There are times, Kate, when one would not think she were a lady but rather a tavern keeper. Be that as it may, I have already learned that a happy farm is a farm that thrives in spite of whatever the Almighty might do with the weather. Our great aunt has put in place such measures as will ensure an income whether there be an excess of rain or drought for there is always something that will be glad of the conditions whatever they may prove to be. I have become almost certain that I am not the only bluestocking in the family for I am sure that Great Aunt has knowledge of a most advanced and peculiar kind in the matters of agriculture and I wonder from where she gets it. What a wise, clever lady and a delightfully improper one she is proving to be; I find I like her very well indeed. Most owners of estates are men and their concerns are much for themselves and their desire to show their tenants who is who in the world and if a shortfall in grain is suffered and with nothing else in place, the tenants are the first to bear the brunt and the estates cannot thrive until a good harvest and we all know that that means a daughter will have to be sold to the highest bidder that money might be had to keep the estate, its servants and tenants afloat. No wonder so many gentlemen gamble their estates away at the tables for want of being rid of the onus which lay so heavily upon them. Alas, so many of them are not raised so as to ensure their good character. Thankfully, dearest Sister, with only two farms to your estate and Mr Cliffton much engaged in city business your girls will not have to endure such an unhappy fate.

I am not entirely sure that Great Aunt was telling the whole truth when she said that Mr Pomphrey was far too unsuitable as well as interfering to take on her rounds for I distinctly heard the very last farmer we called upon mutter to his wife, 'The niece makes a pleasant change from that penny-pinching powdered man-milliner'*. His wife jabbed him full hard in the ribs to silence him but it does rather imply that it has always been Mr Pomphrey's normal duty and I wonder why it was that Great Aunt should engage me upon the task and fib about it but I suppose I am to be left wondering upon the matter.

Having left for our duty calls soon after breakfast and not arriving back at Middlethorpe until the dinner hour of five, I was quite knocked-up* and as tired as a child after a day with a bat and ball and a surfeit of fresh air. My cheeks were a most unbecoming shade of red but thankfully a night's deep sleep has put that parlous state of affairs to rights.

Sadly I fear that as yet there has been no word from Edward but I cannot be sure Mama would have passed such news as my own on to him, though she should for I am still his sister and he my beloved Brother and I yearn so for a single word to put the mind of this your barren and shamed sister at rest. My best love to you and my nieces and nephew.

Your most loving sister,
Athena Cranworth.

****

To Cliffton House

Middlethorpe
Loosmore
Hampshire

September 2nd, 1805

My Dear Sister

I was much relieved to receive your letter this morning and to learn that you are in as good a state of health as you ever were but I was less pleased with its brevity. I suppose I must not be unkind or demanding; if you have had no visitors or have made no visits and everything goes on plainly and without incident, I cannot be so unreasonable as to expect you to invent matters just to fill a sheet of paper, however much it would please me. Still no word from Edward, this is as frightening as it is vexing but I daresay that he will come about anon and be effusive in his assurances that he has been in a whirlwind of pleasurable busyness. I really must cease to think the worst for it gives me headaches now and then and robs me of appetite which is so silly of me especially when you hear what I have to tell you and you will surely not believe it for I cannot believe it myself.

Great Aunt sailed into my bedchamber this morning and began to pull all my gowns from the press* and lay them all about her. She declared the day gowns to be perfectly serviceable if not actually flattering but my dinner and ball gowns which I have not worn since my last Season she declared to be positively passé* although they were she admitted of high quality and well-made and for that reason, should not be thrown out. Can you imagine and were they not of yours and Mama's designing. She has bid Mary rip off all the trimmings from them and to help herself to the furbelows in Great Aunt's collection being much more subtle [her words, not mine]. But first she is to make me a simple, white muslin gown for the Harvest Supper as there is no mantua maker* in the town since the poor woman passed away last winter leaving behind her an unfinished commission.

It seems that whilst at Kestlehurst this event was held in the great barn for the tenants only with Papa and Mama making a brief appearance to drink the health of all; at Middlethorpe, this same event is held in the grand ballroom and we all attend, in fact, most of the county attends. The society ladies are required by Aunt to wear simple gowns that will not put the farmer's wives to shame but we must still be detectable from them and to this end she has suggested that my gown should be embellished with barely visible gold embroidery around the neck, sleeves and hem depicting ears of wheat. I confess it sounds quite beautiful in its simplicity but surely it will make me look as if I am trying to pass myself off as a good deal younger than I am. That is not all. Great Aunt says that my hair, though of good colour and texture, makes me look as if I must have been alive when Queen Anne was on the throne and that I must have it cut short about the front and sides, as is the fashion. At first, I resented all these rather forcefully made suggestions and I made so bold as to ask why I should make all these changes just for a Harvest Supper for I can only wear the one gown for the occasion which will be the new one, which I suppose I must pay for, though I gave the most of what I had to Maudent, to which she replied, "Middlethorpe is a centre of social events. I am known for my dinners and my balls, my picnics held in the grounds and my simple 'at home' evenings when just a few may be present. I had to inform my friends that these occasions would cease for a short while whilst I settle you in, but you can be sure that they will begin again in earnest just as soon as you are content."

Dearest Sister, far from being buried alive as I thought, I am to be more in society than ever I was at Kestlehurst. Oh Kate, I know you must be the outside of pleased for me for it is almost as if I am to have a Season after all. Could it possibly be that that is what Papa intended all along? Had he said something I would not have misjudged him so. But—he did not and therefore, I must conclude in painful honesty that he knows nothing of Great Aunt's lively society. Forgive such ramblings and random thoughts, Kate, for I should perhaps not put them to paper when all else goes so well with me but with who else but you my dearest sibling can I share them. Only imagine, Kate, if you can; I have been here at Middlethorpe so short a time but it is as if the years have dropped away. My complexion has improved and my eyes quite shine as never they did. I had not noticed how dead they must have been until now. So I shall submit to our great aunt's renovations and let us see what we can make of them.

Your loving and most enlivened sister,
Athena Cranworth

****

To Cliffton House

September 8th, 1805.

My own Dear Sister,

What dreadful news you bear me. I must crave forgiveness for my selfishness but it does seem that my happiness is to be short-lived. Mama did not appear to be even remotely unwell when I left Kestlehurst but now you tell me that the doctor believes her to be in a state of permanent illness. If as he has said and I presume this to be Dr Carswell, that he has seen this condition many times why can he not name it, it is most odd of him. Does he perhaps fear that if it should prove to be no such thing that he will be guilty of setting us all about, then I suppose I can understand his professional reticence? And yes, dearest Kate, of course, I will honour your request not to let our parents know that you have told me. It shows something of Papa's much hidden sensibilities that he would not have me worried at such a distance as makes it impossible for me to do anything useful to assist.

Be assured, Kate, that if the worse comes and Mama is to become a long-term invalid as this mystery illness would suggest then I will not do anything to jeopardise my availability to become her nurse and comfort for all that they thought to make my own life a barren waste, for I am still convinced that this is the truth of it. All I ask is that for whatever time that is left to Mama as a fully engaged human being I may be left here to enjoy this interlude for it will be little enough in what may yet turn out to be a long Middlethorpe life for me. Neither would I wish it upon Mama for whatever she has wished upon me. As you quite rightly request, I will say nothing of this to Great Aunt for she would be sure to interfere in the matter on my behalf and therefore, my part in this will remain between you and I until such time as it must become open.

But to happier trivialities; tomorrow we are to go to town to buy the muslin and gold thread for my Harvest Supper gown. It will surely be the last gown that I ever have made, for soon I must be in the matron's cap and fichu*. It seems almost dishonest of me not to tell Mary that there will be no need of her sewing skills in the matter of altering my other gowns. Oh, and yes, I had my hair cut and dressed in the modern manner as Great Aunt wished. She was right, of course, it makes me look quite different and without recourse, to vanity on my part, I fancy it has taken a few years off me. I hope I shall be forgiven if I prove the Belle of the Ball this Harvest, for if all is as you say, it will only be the once.

I remain your affectionate and dutiful sister
Athena Cranworth.

****

To Cliffton House

Middlethorpe
Loosmore
Hampshire

September 12th, 1805

Dearest Katherine,

I am relieved to learn that Mama goes on well and for my own part have managed to appear all cheerful and unconcerned about anything other than our own affairs down here at Middlethorpe. The Harvest Supper Ball is to take place on the 25th of this month when I will meet all our great aunt's friends and acquaintances for the first time.

I find myself quite as excited as a schoolroom miss on her first day out in society. Aunt has a second and much larger kitchen next door to the one that is in permanent use and this is opened on these big occasions and chefs come down from London to assist in the large number of dishes that must be produced from the fruits of the estate. I ventured to inquire of her if she had ever invited Mama and Papa to any of her big occasions as I could not remember our parents ever attending and it would seem that it is some time since she has done so for Mama did not care for the journey and Papa did not approve of a woman running such a big estate and much worse, doing so successfully. When I inquired of her if she had invited them this time on account of my own presence here, she pursed her lips somewhat tightly and just said no but think there was a little more behind that 'no' than was being spoken of. I really do think that Great Aunt is utterly disapproving of our parents' behaviour towards me and quite makes me wonder if there is any point to a female coming of age since it makes little real difference to our lives. Of course, Mama would not be able to travel now anyway but my asking the question was helpful to me in hiding the matter of her condition, whatever that may be, for it is beyond question now that Great Aunt would be most put about at losing me as we are much in friendship and are all support of one another. She takes me much into her every confidence and with the assistance of Mr Pomphrey too who does not seem to mind my inclusion one bit and is quite unprotective of his position. Perhaps all the white lead and rouge cover the cracks of weariness as well as the ones in his countenance for he is certainly the veriest decrepit cockscomb I ever saw.

The business of the estate quite makes my head spin; the reaping of wheat fields and the haymaking go on tirelessly day after day. The orchards are being stripped of their fruits and hives of their honey. Vegetables of every kind are being ripped from the ground and winter crops will be laid. The sheep's coats grow noticeably thicker as winter approaches which seems a way off to us as we enjoy the last of summer's warm breath and the remaining brightness that shines upon us from a sun that still ensures us blue skies for a little longer. I compare the order and contentment we enjoy here at Middlethorpe against that of Kestlehurst and I am afraid I must do it unfavourably. I doubt upon my return home that Papa will listen to me on the matter and he will continue in the old way for it is certain that no woman can be permitted to know about such things, if not Great AM then most assuredly, not me.

Your loving sister,
Athena Cranworth.

****

To Cliffton House

Middlethorpe

September 15th, 1805

Dearest Sister,

I am now inclined to use my own stationery rather than that of the Middlethorpe Estate since you know where I am to be found. Having not heard from you in the last few days I must assume that Mama gives no cause for concern. Had it been otherwise Papa would have written to Great Aunt demanding my release from duty.

Mary really is a treasure and am feeling a little better at losing Gracie but Gracie will always hold a permanent place in my affections and for this reason, I now feel that whatever has taken place at her home in Northumberland the time has come for me to write to her and show my interest in her welfare and that of her family. If her mother died then I think enough time has passed that I may intrude and not too much time has passed as for me to appear careless of our history together. I am quite sad at how things turned about for it was Gracie herself said that she and Maudent were friendly towards one another, [nothing of a romantic nature or improper, of course, Gracie is senior to Maudent by six years and puppies are not to be encouraged even amongst the servant classes] and she might have helped him to learn his letters too. It seems to me that much conspires to keep the servant classes in a state of ignorance, our own family notwithstanding and the church is as guilty of this as any to that end that we will always have servants. Those who cannot read or write or add up numbers are at the mercy of those who can and I find this to be a most un-Christian state of affairs. I will, therefore, write to Maudent to see if he has learnt anything from the books I gave him but, of course, he will have to get someone to read it to him. I think Cook will do so for she must be able to read and write down receipts* and therefore, numbers for weights and the accounts. To know that I have no intention of leaving him to it or not as he sees fit will keep him on his toes in the matter and he will then see in the future how right I was and how much better off he is for it.

My gown is three quarters finished and in the process of embellishment. I think you would be much taken with it and it seems a shame indeed that it might not ever be worn again but that is in God's hands. I will not have to wait until The Harvest Ball to enjoy some society after all, for tomorrow evening we are to have a few of Great Aunt's closest friends for an evening dinner which means at the later hour of eight o'clock. I think she has in mind to introduce me to those who are most important to her on a quieter occasion than attempt to do so under the noisier conditions of a Harvest Ball which is much given over to country dancing and the sort of music heard in taverns and rustic fairs. I am vastly looking forward to it; I believe there will be just six of us at table. I will be sure to write you all about it the very next morning dearest Kate.

Your affectionate sister,
Athena Cranworth.

****

To Cliffton House

My Dearest Kate,

It is midnight but I could not wait till the morning to put pen to paper though I am tired from head to toe. I have had the most extraordinary evening with people who in the normal way of things were so diverse as to be unsuited to find themselves around the same table but nothing is in the normal way of things where Great Aunt M is concerned. Firstly I must tell you of Mr Marcus Temple for he is a Fellow of the Royal Society [and aged thirty years, so Aunt most fervently pointed out to me.] He is the third son of Sir Sedgwick Temple and therefore may look forward to no inheritance but he is in no way bitter against the primogeniture* that puts him in this position for it is certain that no estate can survive without it. He insists that it gave him an edge in the matter of personal ambition and that he is now thankful for it. He is what he calls a permanent student of Natural Philosophy which they now call the Sciences. Great Aunt whispered to me that he is expected to reach the same heights of regard as that of Sir Isaac Newton but she says, he is not so immodest as to tell anyone of this himself, though is all the talk of those who move in his circle of endeavour. As you must remember dear Kate, I ventured to read the works of Sir IN. myself and was so foolish as to quote from him at table which amused one of Papa's chosen suitors and scattered the rest. However, not being easily abashed I have always persisted and Mr Temple was all polite interest in my own and was not in the least shocked or put about by it and was pleased to share some of his findings with me whilst we were all still at table but which had to cease when Aunt's two lady guests began to murmur against the conversation as being unsuitable to their more delicate brains and were at a loss to comprehend how or even why I should be so engaged by it; which brings me to Mrs Winifred Comfort a widow of eighty years and quite the hugest lady I have ever encountered, being a particular friend of Great A M. Aunt sat at head of table of course and Mrs Comfort next to her but how she sat was indeed a miracle for very little of her was on the chair but much of her hanging over each side of it. I do hope you will forgive such vulgarities as I shall now indulge in, Kate, but it almost appeared as if she was sitting astride a fence. Aunt confided later that had she and her friend been alone, she would have provided a far more suitable chair for her but not so in front of others which you must own shows aunt in a most sensitive light that she should leave her friend physically uncomfortable that her pride may be kept comfortably intact. Mrs Comfort it seems had twenty children in her day and became a deal larger with each one. Please take note dearest Kate, for you have always been of such a pretty figure but though you still remain so I could not help but note on your last visit to Kestlehurst a certain plumpness about you that did not appear as if it was only the remains of Baby Cyril and soon to be gone. For your sake alone, Kate, I should hate to see you become Mrs Winifred Comfort. But the lady's size was not her only peculiarity for she twittered like a small cage bird and had so little real conversation that I wonder an intelligent woman such as our great aunt could have any society with her. It seems she was the wife of none other than the great tea and coffee baron, Josiah Comfort who spent so very little time at home but was always on a boat or cutter somewhere in the world inspecting the quality of tea bushes and coffee beans and each time he returned home he left his wife with a little Comfort. I beg you, Kate, do not think that my humour has become course in my advancing years; the jest was that of Great Aunt M and I merely repeat it.

I must to my bed, Kate, for I am falling over this page and may not write another word until morning.

September 17th 10am.

It seems Mrs Comfort is to return today for the noon luncheon as she was much interested in me and wished to meet me under circumstances in which I was not on cue to be fascinating to the company for great aunt's sake. What an interesting observation for one that only appears to twitter but I fear she will be vastly disappointed for there can be no change in me and I am doomed to be fascinating upon unladylike subjects whoever the company

But to continue with my descriptions of our four guests: Miss Marissa Rushworth, who came under the chaperonage of Mrs Comfort and is but ten and seven years of age and not officially out until the Season starts, was placed opposite Mr Temple and a very obvious move it was in such a small party. Miss Rushworth is a considerable heiress having thirty thousand and as you may remember Mr Temple is a third son with nothing but his fame and prospects of more of the same. One would think that her parents would be looking higher on her behalf but I have to tell you that she has the beginnings of buck teeth and it is well-known that once they start on that unfortunate journey they do not stop to consider the feelings of their owner. She is otherwise a pretty girl of average height with dark hair but of course as unschooled as every other schoolroom miss but she plays the pianoforte rather well and Mrs Comfort was much inclined to boast on Miss Rushworth's behalf of her talent for taking likenesses.

I was seated opposite our nearest neighbour, one Sir Simon Lachley, his house being less than a mile from Middlethorpe. There is a lane opposite our entrance fashioned entirely by dint of past use that will take us, if we care to use it directly from Middlethorpe to The Larches. I collect that the Larches is in size and likeness to a parsonage which came as some surprise to me as I am to understand that Sir Simon happily drops Mr Pitt's* name as if they must be close friends but Aunt insists that they are not as Mr Pitt is rather more particular about those with whom he keeps company. Being a man of politics Sir Simon brought much doom, foreboding and indigestion to the table. He considers that the threat of an invasion by the French is still not passed and that that odious little Corsican imitator of true Royalty being such a threat in Austria made me fear for our beloved Edward since Wittenstein is within that region. I find I am also of the mind that Napoleon Bonaparte's ambitions are such that they will keep us all in nightmares for many years to come. How I pity the mothers of sons. Nevertheless, for all the seriousness of his conversation, Sir Simon was much inclined to ogle me in a most ungentlemanlike manner from his side of the table and all the while too which I found a most unpleasant experience. In truth, I could swear an oath upon it that the man was top-heavy* before he even reached our front door which is not the behaviour of a gentleman but Great Aunt informed me this morning that the whole family had long been of that behaviour and much given to the card tables and living under the hatches.* For this reason does Sir Simon live in a house more modest than his position in life.

Now, my final introduction must not upset you dearest, for it is all a lark and nothing more. Lord Robert Westwood, a gentleman of eight and seventy—and he is known by everyone, even the servants as Great Aunt's lover. Being some years younger than her I would have thought him more suited to Mrs Comfort; the profits on tea and coffee are considerable and therefore she has much to offer other than her great proportions. However, it would seem that Lord Westwood has been courting our aunt, or as she would have it, the Middlethorpe estate since he came of age and has never let up on his quest.

We must suppose that he desires to add Middlethorpe to his own rather lesser estate before he dies but Great Aunt will have none of him though it amuses her to have him around, fawning and complimenting and generally playing the beau to her shy Miss. that is, when she is not playing the shameless vixen. It is all most hilariously amusing and I think has quite simply become a habit over the years. He brings her endless bouquets of flowers and posies all chosen with the greatest of care to spell out his messages of devotion and Great Aunt has much diversion in translating them, although I collect that some have been a little rake-ish in their content on those occasions when he is much frustrated by his lack of inroads to her heart, or should that read, the heart of her estate. Interestingly, none of her direct family have ever insisted on her remarrying much preferring to keep Middlethorpe in the family but she is far from happy with the latest prospect in that matter for it seems that it must fall to a great-great-nephew whom she would rather whip than endow. She insists that he is a mutton-head and fit for nothing better than larks and pranks and she supposes that he might be impaired in the brain from birth and if this be the case then Middlethorpe would be sunk within the year and she says that he shall not have it.

The time has passed so quickly that I must leave off now and will write again as soon as more diverting matters present themselves for I am persuaded that Middlethorpe is awash with them and as I say this I see Sir Simon Lachley walking from the house. He was probably presenting his compliments to Great Aunt as is appropriate to a gentleman but, in my opinion, he should be apologising for his unseemly behaviour towards me which would be better appreciated by the 'lightskirts'* to be found at the Vauxhall Gardens*.

Your affectionate sister,
Athena Cranworth.

****

To Cliffton House

Middlethorpe

September 17th, 1805
3pm

My dearest Kate,

I could not wait to return to pen and paper on account of what has since occurred. We were to take luncheon in Great Aunt's private day salon and Mrs Comfort had already been conducted to it by the footman but Aunt pulled me aside at the door and said to me, "I would speak to you on a most important matter when we can be private." I could hardly concentrate on luncheon and on several occasions when Mrs Comfort addressed me, I failed to answer, to which she eventually announced that I was either distracted by love or worry. I allayed her inquisitiveness by saying that the late night had left me tired and inattentive to which I added my apologies. The lady looked somewhat disappointed by my explanation and plainly would have much preferred a declaration of anything at all barring the mundane.

I learned during the luncheon that Mrs Comfort, well-seated on this occasion in a large chair, is a distant relation to Great Aunt and therefore to us also. Upon her own marriage at twenty, she came with her husband to live in the town which is some six miles from Middlethorpe and knowing that she had a relative however distant who had suffered so vilely from so great a loss as both her husband and child within a short time of each other she made herself known and was all Great Aunt Middlethorpe's comfort. Do you suppose one can become inclined to live up to or down to one's name? But it is, for this reason, more than all others that Great Aunt keeps the company of Winifred Comfort for it seems that our aunt is more inclined to count kindnesses than that of irritating personal traits such as twittering and want of intellect and I find this a most reassuringly noble way to be. However, the lady was determined to know all the reason for my being at Middlethorpe and before we had finished the sweet course Mrs Comfort knew as much as I do about my situation. She was much inclined to be on my side in the matter which was encouraging for I am loath to bear ill will where I am wrong to do so. I thought that our guest would never go for I was more eager than is polite to know what it was that Aunt desired to speak of but Mrs Comfort was determined to take a turn around the gardens. Naturally, she uses a stick, if she did not she should surely fall over for her great bosom must also be her greatest enemy and pulls her forward every time she stands. Her ability to walk about the gardens once she is upright and balanced was unexpected and it was full four pm before she departed.

And so, at last, we come to the true reason for this letter. You remember I said that I saw Sir Simon Lachley depart from this house this morning; well, he came on a most particular errand which you will be hard pushed to believe. Great Aunt made no preamble but said, "Sir Simon has asked for permission to make his addresses to you. I said that he must know that since the object of his interest is eight and twenty, neither party is in need of permission but that I thought his suit unlikely to be accepted." At this, Sir Simon became much put about saying that I was already on the shelf at eight and twenty and, therefore, must be grateful for any man's attention as would my parents, who will oblige me to accept. Sir Simon is to return at five thirty this afternoon to invite me to go walking with him and I think it is likely to be up that very lane that goes directly to The Larches. I wonder at it that his opinion of me is so poor as to excite any interest from him, yet according to Aunt, he would have her believe him of being all violence in his feelings. Aunt tells me that he is four and fifty and a widower barely the year. His wife died leaving him childless and he desires progeny before it is too late and therefore, must have a wife a good deal younger than himself but is disinclined to suffer a chit or anyone he would needs must train up to womanly maturity. I can sympathise with him on that deprivation but I think he should be a very poor father indeed preferring to be at the races and the gaming tables and yes, I shall say it for I have always thought myself an astute judge of character, in the stews for that is the sort of man he is, therefore, any attention he is likely to show his children would be of the worst possible example. Oh Kate, if only there had been more time in which I could have sought your advice for I know that I am only here at Middlethorpe for my failure to find a husband and must, therefore, consider Sir Simon's offer but I own, the thought of it fills me with disgust for this violence is not to be found in his affections and all to be found in a quite wanton degree of self-interest.

Ah now, Sister, I will venture to say, 'speak of the devil'. My writing desk being by a window allows me see directly down the front drive and Sir Simon is arrived and in a phaeton* if you please, but with a somewhat imperfectly dressed groomsman. If he thinks that I, who has not as yet even agreed to the walk, should be seen by all and sundry in such a high flying contraption with the likes of Sir Simon, my reputation should at once be tarnished for all time—and if not actually tarnished, then questioned. I think I shall keep him waiting a little, or even a lot; I would not to have him think me eager in any way for his company. In truth, Kate, I am resolved, well, I think I am that I shall not have him at all, for it is I who must live with the wretched creature should I accept him, not Papa. Thank Heavens, the phaeton departs with the groom. It seems that Sir Simon would not have himself too quickly fatigued and preserves all his energy for the walk he proposed. Heavens, this walk is at a late hour and will put dinner back some time I fear, what on earth could be of such urgency in the matter as it could not wait until tomorrow? It is of no use for me to ask you at this point to wish me luck or God's protection for by the time you receive it, it will all be over and I shall be lost to the world either way the penny fall.

Your affectionate sister,
Athena Cranworth.

****

To Cliffton House

Middlethorpe

September 18th, 1805

My dear Kate,

Before I tell you all that occurred during my outing with Sir Simon, I feel I must remonstrate with you over your laxity in the matter of correspondence. You have one governess, three nursemaids and a wet nurse, how can you possibly not find time to write to me, you're most devoted of sisters. If by Papa's request I am not to know of Mama's ill health then you must keep me informed all the same, especially as it is me who is expected to drop my life here at Middlethorpe and return home to care for her at a moment's notice. Papa has written a curt and much to the point note bidding me do as I am required by Aunt and to make myself as amenable as possible; moreover, I am to remember 'what' I am and dress accordingly, having no thought to enhance myself in any way. I find this request—nay— demand, quite extraordinary; one would think that he no longer wishes me to make any kind of marriage and why should he require me to make myself look like one of the servants for I am a Middlethorpe. It is but a month and a half since he was remonstrating with me on the plainness of my dress, now he would have me plainer still. What think you of it sister, do you not also find it particularly odd? You make no mention of Edward since you are remiss enough to mention nothing for want of a letter from you. I find it most strange that we are still in ignorance; does not the government receive despatches in remarkable quick time, even from the foreign battlefield. I think if nothing is forthcoming from either Edward or our parents I shall write to Mr Pitt and inquire of him if he knows of any reason why communications are down between England and Lower Wittenstein. Perhaps I might even ask Sir Simon Lachley if he would make such enquiries for me; that is if he is inclined to do so on my behalf. Indeed I should be much surprised if he was ever to admit knowing me, as I will now explain.

Let me begin by telling you that it was a great mistake on my part to have kept Sir Simon waiting for he was convinced that my purpose in it was to excite his ardour thereby ensuring a proposal. How any man could reach such a conclusion is beyond all reason but I believe gentlemen are much given over to vanity and self-belief which might account for it. I assured him that I had no such intention and that since I am now considered officially a spinster it is a fair assumption that I have never indulged in such behaviour and am entirely innocent of ever exciting any gentleman's ardour but he would not have it and would convince himself otherwise which elicited in me a sincere wish not to embark on the proposed walk with him but I knew that I must. Thus we took our leave of Great Aunt who bore the countenance of one who watches a ship sink and unable to offer any assistance. Having departed the grounds of Middlethorpe for the lane which cuts through farmland, Sir Simon devoted all of the first five minutes to observations of the weather, our surroundings, the straightness of the furrows in this part of the world which I should be able to judge for myself when springtime arrives and in the course of these thoroughly suitable and uninspiring musings I remained resolutely inclined to support myself on my own two limbs without the addition of Sir Simon's arm. But we must remember that Sir Simon is used to handling females as if they were part of his inventory. I, therefore, found my right arm to be suddenly and firmly grasped and put through his and my hand held by his own other hand. I think you must see the picture for it made us appear as a thoroughly married couple. Either that or I had been taken prisoner. I had to think very quickly what my reaction should be. If I should refrain from retrieving my arm, would he see this as an act of encouragement and believe me, Sister, when I say that Sir Simon is one of those men who are easily encouraged for not an indeterminate look is wasted that he will not turn to his purpose; this much I have seen in less than a day of knowing Sir Simon Lachley. If I should regain possession of my arm, would he take this amiss and think me impolite at the very least or a cold fish at worst. If the latter, he would no doubt make it common knowledge and have no scruple in spreading such a rumour; I say this on account of some of his unseemly comments at the table concerning other unfortunate females he has set his cap at. It seems that if they are disinclined to accept his attentions he thinks them either mad or frozen in the virginal state and is wicked enough that he voices such opinions in company, even occasionally attaching a name to them. Think not that I exaggerate sister for already I know of at least six cold fish by name all living somewhere within the vicinity of Pimlico. I, therefore, had to think of something very quickly as not to become a victim of his over-exercised tongue. Thus, I let my reticule* drop from my arm and this required me to release myself from Sir Simon's grip before he could rescue the item for me. By walking a little away from him in order that I might inspect various matters of nature, I was able to keep my arm to myself. Do you not think I did well in the matter? Think not that I did for he spent all his energies attempting to reattach himself to my arm while I manoeuvred all about to resist his efforts until at last he thought it a fine game of chase the hussy. You see now, Kate, such efforts as I made to protect my reputation only succeeded in compromising it. This is how a mere walk with Sir Simon Lachley ends.

The half-mile brought us to The Larches, a modest but fine house and at the moment of our arrival, a very young maid was at the door receiving mail and she looked heavily with child which I thought most exceptional as servants aren't usually permitted to marry. Perhaps she will quit her post when her time comes. Sir Simon seemed to take it as understood that I would enter his house to inspect it and take refreshment but exhausted as I was after so much unwarranted exercise I was at pains to point out to him that as he lived alone except for the servants and I was unaccompanied that this was not the thing at all. That man's reply was as follows. "Come now, madam, don't be playing the coy or the ninny with me. When you chose to come without a chaperone I was entitled to presume upon your own intentions."

To which insult I replied, "Sir, I came without a chaperone on account of your being much in my great aunt's company and a guest in her house over many years that I was entitled to presume that you might at least play the gentleman and could have no intentions of insulting her own flesh and blood."

Making it clear that I would immediately return to Middlethorpe without his arm or indeed his person I turned my back upon him and with near indecent enthusiasm began to retrace my steps down the lane but was followed by further insult which he shouted out at the top of his voice and was clearly heard by a man working in the field opposite who stopped what he was doing so that he might listen. Sir Simon was pleased to bellow, "You, madam, are destined to remain upon the shelf until your last breath, unless that is you manage to snare some wet-goose* of a country clergyman," and thus said he laughed his way to his front door.

As you can imagine, I smarted at such cruel words and I complained bitterly to Great Aunt but was quite shocked at her reaction being either very modern or very much that of the times of her own youth [which history records to have been the outside of disgraceful]. Her response was that Sir Simon whilst most ungentlemanlike, especially towards housemaids, she had to allow him to make his addresses however distasteful they might be to me because of my advanced years. It is common knowledge that ladies of eight and twenty or above are expected to be grateful for any reasonably decent offer on account of desperation, either our own or our parents. Had she refused, Sir Simon would immediately have taken it as a most obvious rejection of himself which would have been followed by his accusing us both of being 'high in the instep'*. Being known for a sharp-tongued gossip, wherever in society his tongue will cut sharpest, he would have had me known on-dit for a bracket-faced tabby* who has been left where she is for any man with any sense of his own happiness knows that it would have been a close call for him should he have been foolish enough to succumb for the sake of a half decent dowry. All this could be expected of him in spite of Great Aunt's hospitality and generosity towards him over the years. I then made a little bold as to suggest that Sir Simon was no longer required to attend The Harvest Supper Ball on account of my own unwillingness to face him ever again. Kate, Aunt's response left me quite aghast, "He shall come to the ball and every other ball and evenings that I shall give because to shun his society would be to precipitate his most cruel of habits and you Athena would become the talk of London at the very least. Furthermore, you should always keep your enemies close to you."

Well, what do you think of that? Could it be that Great Aunt pays a high price in society for being her own person and running her estate herself as if she wore breeches?

Whatever you shall make of it, Kate, I tell you this; over tea and cook's most delicious seed cake we, in our turn, gossiped wickedly about that appalling man a full hour or more until our very late dinner and since you shall have your share of it I will tell you in short. Sir Simon learned his gaming skills from his own father who was already quite heavily in debt at his death which came unexpectedly and a little early at the age of fifty, leaving Sir Simon at the age of four and twenty with a fair estate that had not been wagered and not yet reached entailment to the duns*. By the very age that I am now, he had attained that parlous state and the estate was lost and not a feather to fly with*. Sir Simon was in need of a rich wife but it could be no one of The Ton* since he had lost everything but his title and I do mean everything, for it is difficult for a man to lose his reputation, whereas it is almost too easy for a woman to lose hers but I tell you, Sister, his was so lost, they would not have him in The Ton, title or no title. You may quickly see where with we go in this sister. He was reduced to looking amid respectable trade. There is many a self-made man would have his daughter ennobled by marriage the better to throw off the much-feared label of the 'vulgar mushroom'*. Sir Simon's wife was none other than Clarissa Merchant, only daughter of Nathaniel Merchant the gold and silversmith, for there is trade and there is trade. I believe that much of what they produce stands amid some of the proudest and most noble houses in this and many other lands also. But still, the scar of trade persists [which I confess I find to be a most unsatisfactory state of affairs, for where should the rest of us be without those who deal in trade, though dearest I know you are not inclined to agree].

Aunt has it that Clarissa was a shy and gentle creature much given to hiding in corners whenever the situation would allow and the reason for this was that she was genuinely a pinched-faced girl, utterly plain without a single redeeming feature. Her hair nondescript but generally considered darkish, her eyes were thought to be grey and the worse sin of all, like myself, she was tall but most unfortunately so, in as much as she was a deal taller than most of the young men she was obliged to meet and dance with. So, Mr Merchant resolved to cure the problem once and for all by putting it about that Clarissa came with a fortune of fifty thousand pounds plus two thousand a year for her personal use alone. In other words, whoever married her would become rich overnight and she would never cost him a penny in all her life. Enter Sir Simon Lachley, who it seems made himself so personable as to suggest that he might actually entertain some degree of real feeling for Clarissa Merchant and he was also considered quite handsome in his young days when a surfeit of this, that and everything else did not leave its mark so readily upon either girth or countenance. Clarissa was quickly won and Mr and Mrs Merchant with her on account of their belief that he had chosen Clarissa on her own merits and not that of fifty thousand pounds, plus personal allowance which would leave Sir Simon free to spend her dowry as he pleased and not have to concern himself even about his wife's pin money. With the dowry, Sir Simon bought The Larches so as not to use up too much of his new money too quickly on practicalities, installed his wife and went off back to town to the gaming tables and carousing and very little else. Aunt befriended the reticent and retiring Clarissa introducing her into local society but to no avail. It would appear that Sir Simon's undisguised rejection of her sent her back into dark corners with only her lady's maid for company.

She bore him no children and Great Aunt is bold enough to say that it was unclear whether Lady Lachley was barren or if Sir Simon had chosen not to make much effort in the matter but one thing was certain and that is that Sir Simon does not plough an infertile furrow, as one of his maids at present can testify and many before her. Oh, how naive I am, Kate, for I never thought a moment upon it that he might be the—culprit. I was going to use the term 'father' but it is certain that that man has never been a father to any of his progeny. How I loathe and detest him for it is certain in my mind that Lady Lachley just wasted away and died before her time as she was otherwise in good fettle and apparently not given to ill health in spite of her treatment. She died but a year ago, in truth, not quite the year but we see no evidence of black upon Sir Simon's person and already he looks for another wife. I can only assume that he finds me more to his taste visually if he thinks me up to scratch as a brood mare. You can be sure dear sister that I will never become Lady Lachley the second; I would rather languish a dried up spinster in my own dark corners than submit to such a fate, no matter what Papa or Mama may have to say upon the matter.

Finally, Sister, I have decided to write to Edward on my own account. I can no longer abide by the notion that it may not be done. If it does not reach him, well, there it is and if it does then we must all be the better informed as to the welfare of our beloved son and brother. If necessary, I will write to London demanding to know what goes on but I hope it will not come to that since I am loath to embarrass him in any way. I shall not write to you again until after The Harvest Supper Ball when I am sure I shall have a deal to tell you.

Your truly affectionate sister,
Athena Cranworth.

****

To Cliffton House

Middlethorpe

September 22nd, 1805

My Dearest Kate,

I know I said that I would not write again until after the ball but something has occurred to truly mystify me. It is not an hour since a letter arrived from Papa, indeed it arrived as I was at breakfast, in which he requests that I send any letter I might write to Edward on to Kestlehurst since there is now an arrangement put in place for diplomatic post to be gathered from serving families which will then be transported by means other than the normal postal system and that I must not send any letters to Edward direct as they could be intercepted by the enemy. I would like to know what enemy this is as Bonaparte is at present vexing Austria and not Wittenstein. Furthermore, Wittenstein's problems are civil, between North and South, Upper and Lower and remain entirely within their own borders. That is if I have understood you aright. However, what intrigues me most about Papa's missive is the quickness of its arrival. Forgive me for sounding fanciful dearest Kate, but I know of no special improvements in the business of the post. How could Papa know of my intention to write to Edward and well, it's almost as if you dropped all, taking Cliffton's coach and my letter to Kestlehurst for Papa to read before I should have time to write to Edward. I'm sure this cannot be the case but can think of no other way that it might have been managed. You must write to me, Kate, and ease my mind that there is nothing that is being hidden from me, for it does seem to me that there is much I do not know and would know why it is that I should be kept in ignorance. Have you perhaps heard that Edward is in some sort of danger—or worse and seek to keep it from me?

Your affectionate sister,
Athena Cranworth.

****

To Cliffton House

Middlethorpe

September 26th, 1805

My Dearest Kate,

Thank God you wrote me so swiftly; as you may imagine, it arrived well before I was up to receive it for I have kept late hours this morning for good reason. I apologise unreservedly for my most lunatic of outbursts but I would beg you comprehend that I am much out of the family save for Great Aunt and feel it so. I allowed my imaginings to get the better of me and at such a moment one may put two and two together and come to a most wicked five as a result. I am almost delirious with relief that no ill news is come concerning Edward and no, of course, you would not keep it from me if it should and why should it. As you say he is safely tucked up in his Ambassadorial office and should he, in all haste, need to depart the country, he would be given safe conduct. Moreover, you are right as usual dearest Kate; coincidence is a very strange thing indeed, in truth, much mystery may be attached to it. Why should not Papa think that I might take it into my head to write to Edward, albeit that I was asked not to for it is certain that he believes me to be incapable of pleasing him in anything, let alone the obedience owed by a daughter, even one who is well past being of age but he is only too aware of my great love for my brother but be not envious my dear sister for my love for you is equal to it.

And now that I am truly humbled into profuse apologies please let us turn to brighter and happier matters. The last few days have been quite the busiest I have ever known. As well as all the arrangements for the ball the repair work on the tenants' cottages has begun in earnest as I understand from Isaac, the head gardener, that autumn is to be expected early this year and will arrive blowing its own trumpets. Isaac is never wrong I am told and therefore, I pass this information on to you to be taken to heart. You have but two tenants to trouble your purse and it behoves you to ensure that they will see the winter through dry and warm. It will be all the better to your credit to be known for a kind mistress who cares for those at her mercy. Though I have said that I would never write to him again I shall inform Papa the same and I do hope that he will do likewise. I have said it before but I will risk repetition in saying that it is certain that the longer repairs are left the more expensive they become. I repeat myself for it is much known that our family is disinclined to tenant expenditure yet equally distraught in having to pay out upon the results of such disinclination.

The servants quarters here are full to the roof with London chefs and their own minions who came to manufacture the harvest feast. Our cook Mrs Willows greets them as old friends and all go on so cheerfully and without professional rancour as to be unique. One can only think that this is Great AM's magic again for she does seem to have a most positive effect upon all who fall beneath her feet. All the Middlethorpe gardeners were brought in to decorate the ballroom in the manner of The Harvest. Only imagine, Kate, there were sheaves all around the room and great garlands of fruits and vegetables strung together all about and draped around the table that reaches almost the length of the room. At the end of the night's festivities, all the garlands and sheaves are distributed back amongst the tenants so none goes to waste. Isaac and his boy strip their artistry before all and even some of the gentry, including the ladies, join in with it and is a recognised part of the finale to the night's celebrations. All becomes quite raucous and by the end everyone is utterly knocked-up. Imagine my surprise when I saw that every one of the guests from amongst the tenants arrived at the ball with an empty basket. I was eventually to discover that each basket is filled with whatever delicacies have not been consumed during the course of the evening.

Aunt's society friends danced with the tenants and believe me when I say that not one of our rough-handed sons of the soil was too shy or reticent in asking a grand lady to take the floor with them and many a rosy-cheeked farmer's wife stepped out with a gentleman of consequence and all were easy with one another on account of it being long in practice. Papa and Mama would have been shocked to their very core and may have much more to do with the lack of an invitation than Aunt owned to. But before I go on to tell you of the evening's events I simply must tell you how well I looked in my new gown. Oh Kate, I can't begin to describe to you how beautiful it was. A simple concoction of sarcenet* over muslin; I entered the ballroom on Aunt's arm as she was officially presenting me to her society. There were some genuine gasps of admiration as I entered. Of course, there were no jewels of any matter as Great A doesn't like anyone to outshine the more humble guests but she did lend me a pair of gold earrings that looked like tiny bells at the end of an almost invisible gold chain and the golden embroidered ears of wheat on my gown served for the rest of my jewellery, I assure you I was the very essence of modest understatement yet the whole stood out amongst them all, in fact, for my eight and twenty years I looked almost maidenly. There is something to be said, though not a great deal, for the mature years as we are over the problems of skin blemishes that erupt overnight, to the horror of their recipient and their mamas and for which there is no useful disguising. I overheard Mrs Comfort remark to a lady of her intimate acquaintance that she thought me much in looks. Dearest sister, I think it the first time I have ever heard that said of me and you must forgive me if I bask in it a little while longer, for it was said of you often and can still be thought true. I have in consequence given Mary a simple necklace of mine, you must remember it, the amber and coral one, as a thank you to her for contriving to make me appear so beautiful and I have grown quite used to my new and modern hairstyle. Really, Kate, you would not know me.

Mr Pomphrey arrived on the scene resplendent as usual in finery quite thirty years and more out of date, all most exquisitely embroidered which could be said to be against Aunt's rules but everyone is used to Mr Pomphrey and he gets away with it. Nevertheless, she sent him back to his quarters to correct himself because she said, and here you must forgive me the use of a certain vulgarity not considered to be known to ladies although I give you all assurance that it is not my own, that he was wearing more cosmetics than the ladies and she said he looked like a 'Molly House clown'*. One quite wonders these days how it was that gentlemen got themselves up in such a fashion [even gentlemen like Mr Pomphrey and all considered quite normal at the time], even for those who did not frequent the M H. I tell you, Kate, the paintings of our forebears that hang upon the walls of Kestlehurst do not do justice to the reality.

But now to the all-important business of the dancing; there were twelve musicians in all who come every year as a standing arrangement to the Middlethorpe harvest and to be sure, they put up quite a noise between them and are much admired for their command of country music and the more refined alike which serves all. My first partner for a locally known dance which I had to be taught by Mary, and called The Gathering into Sheaves, was our Head Gardener's boy Simeon. Being just sixteen years old, I think Aunt engaged him to my service, for this dance is something to behold and would never be tolerated by Mama or Papa; it is a riot of movement danced in a great circle where the females are thrown up in the air and must be caught by the next male along in the circle before they hit the floor. To avoid any impropriety, she must be caught at the waist at a half or full arm's length according to muscle strength whereupon she is spun round to face the opposite way being the outside circle and the gentleman is now inside. The gentleman's circle then moves a pace to his left if he is inside and to his right if he is outside, to face the next lady. After a little footwork by both parties, the whole goes on in the same manner until one is returned to one's original position and partner, much as all dances.

Above a certain age, one is not expected to participate and it has to be said that ladies above a certain weight would be frowned upon should they attempt it for it is a matter of truth that a young gentleman seeing the approach of any degree of ampleness would be in extremity of anguish the nearer she got, knowing that in order to prevent the most physical of disasters befalling them he would be obliged to forget the half or arm's length rule and both likely to end up red-faced and in such close proximity as to cause a scandal; but sister, did you ever hear of such a dance? Well, as you may imagine it was the cause of a deal of noise and shrieking for there is a genuine fear that if they are not caught, the females will land heavily and sprain an ankle or even worse, break it. I have been assured though that this dark prophecy has never yet been realised. This dance is always first for it breaks down barriers that may have arisen during the course of the year with its guaranteed precipitation into mildly strident behaviour. I think the young men who are expected to dance this set for the very first time must be in agonies of worry over it the night before and heaven help the partner of he who moves to the left instead of the right but I collect that the young ladies are ever excited at the prospect of being thrown up into the air; I can assure you sister that after the Gathering into Sheaves, no one is left standing on ceremony and after a short interval during which much-needed refreshments were taken there followed the first Cotillion.

The ballroom at Middlethorpe, even when filled with small tables, many chairs and the great feast table which is pushed over to the outside wall, there is still enough room to make up three sets of dancers without risk of collision, this will give you some idea of its grandeur [as well as the number of candles required to light it.] It was with some surprise that I accepted Mr Temple's request to take my hand in the first Cotillion for I was still so flushed from Gathering into Sheaves that I had quite forgotten how much I was in looks. Mr Temple turned out to be a fine dancer which one tends not to expect of the absentmindedness of natural philosophers but it seems he is as much a man of this world as he is of the 'Isle of Cerebral' and we talked much during the dance whereupon he thought to tell me that he could foresee a time in the future when all our city streets will be lit with gas. Only imagine it, Kate, no dark corners for the likes of footpads to hide. I asked him many questions during the course of the dance, one of which was, did he know anything about electricity and its likelihood of proper application. He cast me a look which I have not yet quite fathomed but which probably had its origins in either shock or disapproval but he nevertheless made me an answer. He said that he was much surprised that I had even heard of it other than in the context of lightning storms and quack medics but that it was unlikely to have any impact on us in our lifetime and was something much in the future. My question, however, did not give him a disgust of me enough to prevent him from seeking me out for a second dance after which Aunt warned me that I must not accept a third. Did she not think that I had been through enough Seasons not to remember this rule? Now I think of it, if I had ever had a third* chance with anyone I would not now find myself in this situation and would be otherwise occupied with my own brood as you are dear Kate.

But it is of no consequence for it was at this point in the proceedings our final guest arrived, Lady Maud Bonnington-ffrench, daughter of Earl and Countess B-ff of Penchester a considerable heiress as one might assume of twenty years and obviously taking their time in choosing a husband for it is certain she may have the pick of the best so long as the best are present and in circulation. Such a beauty was never seen I think, for her complexion was of the most perfect, an almost unreal concoction of peaches and cream with strawberry lips [that may have owed something to cosmetic assistance]. Her hair was of that golden hue which bears something of the sunset hidden amongst its threads that fringed eyes of pure azure and all that remained to be judged was so perfectly proportioned as to have all the gentlemen cast their eyes upon her and the sons of the soil blushing into their clean white shirts. You will by now be bursting for me to describe Lady Maud's gown for no doubt you will be expecting it to be above all others designed to stand out, much against all Aunt's rules. Well, Sister, it stood out very well indeed for in simplicity it outdid my own in all its composition. Plain white muslin, that was it, plain white muslin but most perfectly cut, not a bit of sarcenet to be seen, just a few strategically placed white satin ribbons and one other tied about her hair. As to jewels, the only ones to be seen were the blue sapphires in her eyes. She knew very well the figure she cut and arrived late to make sure that she would be seen to full advantage by all and I suspect, to avoid the levelling effect of the Gathering into Sheaves. She appeared to be most modest and unassuming concerning her effect but I think she was thoroughly aware of it and had been much schooled in acting the part of the innocent in possession of great treasures. She may wait as long as is practicable and still have queues at the door. It is no surprise therefore that Mr Temple could be seen dancing with her later that evening, most purposefully introduced to her as he was by Aunt. What likelihood, therefore, was there of a third dance. I quickly forgot that I was 'in looks'.

Miss Marissa Rushworth, chaperoned by Mrs Comfort, as usual, looked fetching in sprigged muslin and the two of them tittered their way through the entire event while Aunt tut-tutted that the girl would be old before her time if she didn't gather a wit or two before she reached eight and ten, which she was not likely to do if she kept too much company with Mrs Comfort whom she secretly thinks is retreating back into the nursery these last two years. Naturally, being much in company with her at

Middlethorpe Mr Temple danced with Miss Rushworth and I think she is developing quite a tendre for him. I daresay he sees it and will divert her away from his approaching middle-age but there again, he may not.

Now, here you will surely laugh fit to burst for Sir Simon Lachley had the effrontery not only to attempt to engage me upon the dance floor but that that dance should be a Quadrille. As you can testify dearest Kate, I have never mastered the complexities of the Quadrille and I am not alone in this failure. You, of course, dearest were quite remarkable at it and who can forget that many ceased their own attempts upon it to watch yours but for Sir Simon to imagine that at his age and girth and ungainly gait he could manage such a dance, well, I almost forgot my manners but I was bold enough to say that I not only thought it unwise for him to attempt it but that he could hardly marvel at it that I did not mean to dance any dance with him. You must not think I embarrassed him before all for I stated every word very quietly that none should hear and he should not feel entitled to avenge himself upon either Aunt or me in a London coffee-house.

Great A's perennial suitor brought a Commander of Dragoons with him some of his men who looked very handsome and caused much interest amongst the young ladies and the tenant's daughters. I have to tell you that I approached the Commander by the name of William Westphaharn, a most unusual name do not you think and I asked him what he knew of the troubled situation in Wittenstein. His reply has left me much perplexed for he said that other than the rumour concerning the Prince of Lower Wittenstein's health and the lack of an heir at present he knows of no other matter that should cause any concern for our brother. He did, however, mention a relative of the prince in Upper Wittenstein, Rodolphe von Witten who would be likely to take over both cantons if the prince should die, also that he is much disliked by both cantons but other than that the country is at peace, at least whilst Bonaparte is busy elsewhere. I think, therefore, dearest Kate, that you may have been on the receiving end of something approaching a Banbury story* but thank God for it, that it is so, enabling me to enjoy the rest of the ball to the fullest extent with neither concern nor guilt.

There must have been between three and four hundred guests and I found myself to be much introduced to the highest personages in the county and well beyond and wondered how many of those not overnighting at Middlethorpe would find their way home for it is certain that the inn in Loosmore could not begin to lodge them all but I will tell you of these another time.

This has been a most extended letter dearest Kate and I close for now, as you will know I must shortly expect my dance partners to arrive to address me with their nosegays.

Oh, Kate I am so unused to these procedures for I was much overlooked in every way during my Seasons. You found them mostly tedious except for the beaux you much admired but I am inclined to treasure them all. Those of us so unused to compliments cherish every one. You have ever been all kindness enough not to mention it but I know that you remember too well that even in my bloom I had so few offers for the dance floor whilst you were barely ever off it that even Sir Simon's attentions are a compliment in their own way but none shall come much longer. Autumn arrives soon for me, Kate, and will be shorter than winter I fear.

There is much more to tell you dearest but it must wait for another day. Take care as the days shorten; life is precarious and health precious.

From your devoted sister,
Athena Cranworth.

****

To Cliffton House

Dearest Kate,

I apologise for the maudlin ending to my last letter which was
collected shortly after I had sealed it and left it in the hall else I
should have retrieved it and scratched out those last words. I'm
not sure what came over me but an ill wind blew across my bows
and I felt a storm brewing yet I am so happy, happier than I have
ever been in my life, save for the possibility that it may be
brought to an end by Mama's condition. I do hope that does not
sound too selfish of me. My days with our great aunt are full of
usefulness and learning and there can be no earthly reason for
my presentiment. In the last hour, Aunt has bid me dispense with
Middlethorpe and address her as Great A Horatia, does that not
bode well for our burgeoning closeness. Far from being buried
alive here, I was buried alive at Kestlehurst and did not know it.
But enough of this grey mood; my beaux came to call as is
customary and we served them refreshments and they presented
their posies. Great A and I have had much diversion in translating
their meanings. Some are politely gracious and others quite
gushing in their declarations and cannot be taken seriously for it
is certain that having presented them to me today they will wish
they could retrieve them tomorrow but oh what fun, Kate, what
delicious contentment—if it wasn't for these feelings that
suddenly plague me so.

We are to have our friends around the evening dinner table again tomorrow. I am sure it will be as it was before and nothing of any moment to report, so now I will leave it a few days before I write again, especially as my right hand quite aches from having written so much today but please feel free to bother me with all that bothers you darling Kate.

Your loving sister,
Athena Cranworth.

****

To Cliffton House

Middlethorpe

October 1st, 1805

My Dearest Sister,

I said I would leave off writing to you for a few days and I have kept my word but now I have more to tell you. Our small dinner party which I told you of had an extra guest, well, two actually counting the chaperone. Mrs Comfort attended and as usual brought Miss Marissa Rushworth who has offered me the privilege of addressing her by her Christian name as I am older than her by eleven years. Lord Westwood, Aunt's suitor, Mr Temple and sadly Sir Simon who was thankfully put opposite the chaperone a Miss Peerless of whom I shall tell in a moment. I was a little surprised to find that Miss Rushworth was placed opposite myself which seemed to please her not, in spite of her invitation earlier to use her first name. But, to our surprise, the guest who was placed opposite Mr Temple was none other than Lady Maud. I collect she is come into Loosmore to visit her grandfather this last month who lives some ten miles from Middlethorpe. Aunt issued the invitation to take dinner with us during the course of the Harvest Ball. Mr T did not take his eyes from her the while but she did look so wonderful in a blue gown of velvet that echoed her eye colour, azure if you recall.

I do believe that Aunt is attempting to arrange an alliance between Mr Marcus Temple and Lady Maud. We must not forget that though he is to be the victim of primogeniture and poor by comparison as a result, his family is of consequence and he, of course, a man of stature in his own right as a Fellow of the Royal Society; I, therefore, think that Aunt is engineering him a much-needed fortune but if it works, he will have a poor deal of it other than the money; she comes with forty thousand, if you can be brought to imagine such a sum. She does not twitter like Miss Rushworth but I fear her head is only turned by herself, especially when passing a mirror—large or small. My fears, therefore, on Miss Rushworth's behalf must be taken seriously for it is certain that with the likes of Lady Maud in the arena the Miss Rushworth's of this world, even with thirty thousand can have not hope lest he fall blindingly in love with her which is unlikely I assure you. The problem being, apart from her twittering and burgeoning teeth, the former of which she might have caught from Mrs Comfort and may yet be cured, that she is just seventeen. Now I know this is not so unusual, there are many marriages based upon a middle aged man's unworthy desire of young flesh and where there is a want of money or title such arrangements are far from exceptional but the thing is, Mr Temple is a man of advanced knowledge and much given, as all his kind to shutting himself away in his thoughts a good deal of the time. Between being shut away in town in The Royal Society and being shut away in his head when at home, if he has a wife at all, he will forget who she is for months at a time unless she have something of particularity with which to oblige him to remember her and should they be of Lady Maud's or Miss Rushworth's characters, he will likely forget them entirely for the simplest of reasons, neither Lady Maud or Miss Marissa Rushworth will have a single thought with which to engage him. Miss Rushworth would twitter him right out of their front door and Lady Maud would have him admire her from every angle until he could bear the sight of her no more and she would be forced to find some other gentleman to admire her.

Do not, I beg you, think that I come to these conclusions lightly or out of misplaced envy, for something was said at the dinner table for which I do not feel entirely without responsibility. Your wretched sister would engage Mr T in some intellectual conversation, as is my wont for I was sorely tried by the small talk that is considered proper on these occasions. Try as she might, Aunt made a stab at the military situation which had Sir Simon blustering happily but uselessly on the subject for Bonaparte has not succeeded in invading us so thankfully there was less to talk about. As you might expect apart from our great aunt, the ladies present were of little mind to speak on such matters. Miss Peerless, a most unfortunate name given the creature that bore it, insisted that she did not want her lamb troubled by such wickedness as perpetrated by the likes of those dreadful foreigners. Lady Maud pretended to pacify her troubled maiden aunt [I collect a disinherited relation on her mother's side] whilst making out that she was perfectly able to contend with the horrors of what might be ahead of us but it was only meant to impress the gentlemen for almost without drawing breath she was quick to inquire if we had seen the new bonnets in Madam Modiste's, the milliners in Loosmore. Mrs Comfort desired to know if there was any more cauliflower to be had and Miss Rushworth stared vacantly at her plate. As there was to be no more forthcoming on that most imminent of matters being Bonaparte I brought Mr Temple's occupation to the fore and begged him tell us more of the great enlightenments that are being realised from within the walls of that august society and that he might be persuaded to bring us the privilege of pictures of those verminous creatures that directly infest our lives and are too small to be ascertained by the naked eye and even the true condition of human skin neither of which can be seen in true detail save by the eye of Mr Robert Hook's wondrous microscope.

Sir Robert Westwood was outraged, saying that human skin was a most unsuitable departure for the dinner table and vermin of the particular kind as I was indelicate enough to mention with ladies present even more so and was obliged to make his apologies to Aunt for his opinion of my preferences in conversation which was no doubt a blind for his opinion of me. He went on to say that, "Such things were acceptable in the salon where ladies of the bluestocking inclination preside alongside gentlemen of knowledge but for true ladies, such discourse was beyond the pale of decency."

Aunt had quite a cunning look in her eye at all this going on around her table and demanded of Sir Robert which class of female he thought her to fall into. Sir Robert was much flustered by this question and blustered on a little until he suddenly alighted upon the very answer, "You, ma'am, are of an age when all privileges are grantable." It was easy to see that while Aunt appreciated the relative quickness of wit that came up with the answer she was not so enamoured of the answer.

Mrs Comfort then came about with her opinion on the matter which was that no gentleman could ever be desirous of a wife that knew anything for it would make him feel much discomposed of his own position.

Sir Robert and Sir Simon were a good deal comforted by her opinion as were certain others around the table but I was not for I ventured to say that, only a stupid man could be in want of a stupid wife. Oh sister, if only you could have been there to hear the silence that fell upon the table. Yet Aunt had the look of a cat who had spied sport and Mr T once again cast me a glance I was not able to determine the nature of. When the silence could contain itself no longer uproar ensued. Sir Robert, Mrs Comfort and Miss Peerless were much overset with Sir Simon ill-naturedly pronouncing that this is what comes of letting females read books and Miss Peerless insisting that no charge of hers was ever permitted to read a book that would give any gentleman cause for concern. At this, Mrs Comfort had to go one better by stepping down the ladder of reading achievements by assuring us all that she never read anything more taxing than *The Ladies Magazine* and *The Morning Post* and Miss Rushworth continued to look at her plate. Aunt looked on silently smiling all the while though I was hard put to tell what she had to smile about. Please note dear Kate that Mr T passed absolutely no comment but rather he invited Aunt and myself to accompany him in a sennight's time to a public lecture at The Royal Society. Now, what do you think of that? I am beside myself with joy and excitement at the prospect but Lady Maud was so put out as to momentarily forget to pose her fine profile and Miss Rushworth looked up from her plate.

Mr T said that the public lectures are filled with ladies desirous to know more of the world that they inhabit and that any of the ladies around the table were welcome to join the party. Sir Simon harrumphed that it was a great mistake to let females know anything they don't need to and it would be far better if The Society gave the seats to men who knew what to do with such knowledge, to which I replied, quite forgetting the threat of the coffee-house that in that case, he had probably never attended such a lecture. Aunt, by now fearing a riot in her dining room, all alas incited by your rattle* of a sister bade the ladies retire to the drawing room for coffee and leave the gentlemen to their port. I think much must have been said once we ladies were out of hearing distance but as yet I cannot tell what it was. You know only too well, Kate, how I hate it when we have to leave the men to their port for when we are just ladies, all meaningful conversation ceases as a rule and this occasion was certainly no exception. I was much advised by Mrs Comfort and Miss Peerless against any further interest in affairs that can only bring me to grief and that if I must continue to be so unladylike then to keep it to myself for if I did not I would be held in disgust by society in general and gentlemen in particular. I'm afraid, Kate, the disgust was all mine and I said that I had no intention of obliging anyone but myself in the matter and that I had long been held in such disgust and was by now entirely used to it. I was made to feel their disapproval although after a moment or so of tutting it was held silently. Eventually, when the gentlemen re-joined us, all was cheerful although I had the distinct feeling that that had more to do with the imbibing of port than the conversation they engaged in which undoubtedly was a continuation of what had gone before. Turns were taken at the pianoforte, a few songs were sung and we even managed a country dance or two without bruised feelings transferring themselves to my toes. You must be in despair of me Kate for as you see, though it be forever to my own detriment I do not— cannot alter but for all that this is true, when they were all departed Aunt took up my hand and patting it she said, "You really did awfully well my dear; I was most proud of you." Although I know Aunt to enjoy being a little disreputable this was not the reaction I had been expecting and I went to my bed much perplexed by it and pondered it unsuccessfully for some time. Then just before the curtains of sleep dropped, I wondered how it was that Aunt comes to know Mr Temple and how he comes to be so much in her society even if he does live in the nearby town of Loosmore when not in London. No doubt I shall learn the answers to these things anon but in the mean time I remain—

Your loving and devoted sister,
Athena Cranworth.

****

To Cliffton House

Middlethorpe

October 9th, 1805

My Dearest Kate,

My heart gladdens with relief to hear your health remains robust and that little Cyril has stopped screaming at last. It was far too early for teething so I must assume that having come in from that place where his divine little soul was fashioned he thought a deal less of where he found himself, that is to say a world where the likes of Bonaparte tramples over foreign thrones and even yet casts his greedy and envious eye upon our own; all I can say is God Save the King and Admiral Lord Nelson and little Cyril will come round to it all in time, as we all must.

I have yet to tell you that the long gap between this letter and the last was because I took chill the very night of my last writing to you and was forced to retreat to my bed. It was one of those change of season fevers that beset us all when autumn elbows summer from the scene and Aunt was obliged to send out for Hungary Water* to relieve my dismal headache that throbbed first one side then the other and finally on top of my poor head which exploded with a furnace of heat while the rest of me shivered in complete denial of the warming pans that filled my bed. For the rest of my curative course, I relied on Isaac's fine borage honey and lemons. I was much relieved that Aunt did not call out Dr Worth to subject me to the leeches for I do not think they draw out the ague at all and it seems neither does she; we do see eye to eye, she and I, on so many matters which is the best of boons to those who share a roof.

Mr Temple was kind enough to risk his own health by coming to visit me and he sat with me a while [with Mary in attendance, of course, for I was in my nightrail*] and was most upset at the thought that I might miss The Royal Society lecture. I am resolved not to disappoint either Mr Temple or myself for it is quite evident that he much desires me not to be deprived of this event and to attend even if I am breathing my last. We had a little tea party in my bedchamber for which Aunt joined us although in acknowledgement of her age she sat well away from me and quite hugged the fireplace but we were very merry and it much served to relieve me of my symptoms. Is it not a marvel that love and kindness and generosity of heart and spirit may do more miracles than Hungary Water*, Hartshorn* or any of those other sovereign remedies the apothecary is pleased to drive down our throats without a second thought for what it might do to our health.

I am happy to say that in spite of the long journey to London and the continuance of my indisposition I attended the lecture and though rather pale, apart from my red nose I was over the worst. I'll not burden you with the facts of the journey, it passed like any other at this time of year, tedious and draughty, which could have set me back but I was wrapped in blankets the whole way with Aunt and Mr T checking the temperature of my hands every other mile and hot bricks at my feet. He was also most vocal with the keepers of the coaching inns on the matter of damp beds for which as you know some are infamous, once summer is gone and linen becomes more difficult to get dry. In one inn, in particular, the servants were suddenly to be found in mine and Aunt's rooms with warming pans while steam rose from our beds like swamp gas which conspicuously proved his point. Had he not undertaken this course of action I fear I should have succumbed to the very worst inflammation and congestion of the lungs and passed out of this world far from home; in which momentary indulgence in self-pity I fancy would have brought all Papa and Mama's troubles to an end.

I can't begin to tell you how wonderful the lecture was, Kate. Great A was in a veritable transport of enthralment as was I. I know you have never interested yourself in such matters but you should have seen Mr T when he stepped up upon the dais to explain the proposed workings of a street gas mantle and the very manner of production of the gas in such vast quantities that would be needed to reduce the dangers of the city street at night forever. Thus the early difficulties resolved it would only be a matter of time before gas would enter everybody's homes to the betterment in health and general wellbeing of all. Only imagine, Kate, having hot water next our bedchambers that our poor servants would no longer need to carry pails and jugs up the stairs. A boon to all indeed I think and I pray for its swift arrival. I will spare you the details of this particular science as I know you will not bother to read them and I must confess to some difficulty of my own in bringing to recall all that was said upon it as my head was not entirely returned to me though I made all attempts in concentration to offset the fog that persisted in my brain but this which I have to tell you now must surely engage even you with all hope, Kate, for in the field of medicine, I heard Mr Temple whisper to another gentleman of the society that he had heard of a successful attempt upon opium in the isolating of something proposed to be called morphia which it is believed will so mask pain as to render it gone entirely from the physical senses. That it was whispered and not to me tells me they sit upon it in secrecy I think as it is not amongst their own achievements and its usage must be a long way off, much as proper street lighting but you must own that both are miracles of scholarship and bode so very well for the lives of your children. Not so our poor dear soldiers and seafaring men I fear; how I could weep for their sufferings.

Oh dearest Kate, the winds blow hard just as Isaac said they would but fancy I hear cries carried upon them and a cold draws inwards and around me. I know you will say that the fever has brought me to low spirits but you know I had this feeling before I succumbed to the chill.

Did I mention that I have written to Edward as I said I would?

Your loving sister,
Athena Cranworth.

****

To Cliffton House

My Dearest Kate,

I am in want of understanding your silence, knowing how unwell I have been I should have expected you to be all concern. But perhaps I am being cruel and unfair dearest; have you perchance suffered likewise. Children are so apt to be the first to fall for these things and they pass them around the household like personal gifts, I do hope this is not the case. In my new incarnation even my physiognomy is not much destroyed by the ravages of the fever but you, my most beautiful of sisters, would take it badly for the slightest impairment shows upon your countenance. I declare you will be a great beauty right to the end, for yours is carried in your bone structure rather than the tone of your face which must always collapse with the passage of time. How fortunate Cliffton is, I hope he never needs to be reminded of it. There, I have both reprimanded and embraced you handsomely in the space of a small piece of paper, I hope I am forgiven.

Now I must bring you some amusement for Aunt had her friends to dinner again last night. Lady Maud and Miss Peerless did not attend which surprised me not a little bit at all. I think Lady Maud found it difficult to pose and eat at the same time, especially when the conversation went so against her and Miss Peerless's inclinations but Sir Simon brought a guest; I will describe her as a lady friend rather than a lady. Aunt said that she thought it a rebound in the face of my utter rejection of him. Although charitable as I am disposed to be with most people, I would have to say that if he thought to better me or even equal me with his new choice, I should take it very ill indeed. Her name is Mariah Brindle and must be about fifty years at a generous guess and she has been a widow less time than he has been a widower, thus far they share an equality of shamelessness. Neither was she in black or mourning mauve though Mr Brindle is only deceased these six months. She came dressed in a most noisy copper and rust coloured confection with a matching turban supporting ostrich feathers in various shades of autumn. From beneath the turban appeared an abundance of hair of a similar red colour which clashed outrageously, the whole giving the lady an appearance of being on fire. As to the lady herself, I noticed a certain tightness of vowels as if she were reining them in by force and much against the comfort of habit. There is no doubt in my mind that she is looking for a billet above her usual station and I am inclined to wish her luck in the matter.

If it is considered acceptable for those in society to step up where they are not born then I do not see why the likes of Mrs Brindle may not do so for it is certain that Sir Simon is a carouser and an above age rake and, therefore, is undeserving of a lady of quality or moral standing. If anyone can handle the likes of Sir Simon, I would declare Mrs Brindle the most appropriate of candidates. I can say this because, in a moment of privacy, Aunt wheedled the truth out of him. Mrs Brindle is none other than the landlady of The Olde Nag, a public drinking establishment only just on the right side of The East End of London which informs us all of Sir Simon's preferred watering holes. Aunt was not asked to supply her with a room for the night and there was no arrangement made to conduct her to the inn in Loosmore, therefore, we must assume she spent the night at The Larches with only the servants in attendance, one of whom is large with Lachley. Though it was vastly improper of him to have brought such a person to Aunt's table I think his intentions must be honourable for him to have done so, but her conduct was much as the rest of her thus his peers will surely object most vociferously and therefore doubt that Mrs Brindle is like to become anything more than Mrs Brindle. She actually picked up her chop bones with her hands and sucked so hard upon them leaving nothing for the dogs which Sir Simon thought a fine game and immediately made to join her in the practice fully expecting us all to participate, I suspect the better to make Mrs Brindle feel comfortable whilst the rest of us felt extremes of discomfort on her behalf although I must assure, not on Sir Simon's.

Miss Rushworth, who was made to sit next to the object of her intentions, made a concerted effort to engage Mr T in conversation, that is to say, after Mrs Comfort's considerable right elbow found its target in the girl's ribcage. It was quite obvious to me that in order to steal a march on my own undisguised interest in matters of science and invention Mrs Comfort had been schooling her in what questions to put to Mr T without going too much against her previous censure of me but that the girl had no understanding of her own question was painful to watch and his answer was greeted with a tremulous "Oooh." The question that Miss Rushworth was pleased to put to him was, 'what is our world made of', to which his answer was to reel off the table of many chemicals thus far discovered and which he assured us are but the tip of an iceberg.

Miss Rushworth thanked him prettily but retreated hastily to the pattern on her plate and did not speak again until she was pleased to avail us of the rumour that Mrs Phillips has not paid her butcher in a year nor her candle bill in eight and ten months, Mrs Phillips being the wife of the Member for Loosmore. Now henceforth neither trader will deliver further until the bills are paid. Sir Simon was much engaged in this bit of news and would glean every detail that Miss Rushworth was pleased to embroider and he was resolved to prod Phillips on the matter seeing as how they had never got on and Mr Phillips had been much inclined to criticise Sir Simon on a number of matters which Sir Simon did not see fit to illuminate us. Is it not dispiriting dearest sister when people are more inclined to the world of gossip than the knowledge the world has to offer us? It is with some shame that I have to admit that our own sex is much to blame in this but perhaps it is caused by want of useful purpose—which is denied us. As usual, Aunt watched and listened more than she spoke and that glint in her eye which I now have become so used to, was much in evidence. I wonder if I shall ever learn what it is that goes on in her mind and I wonder too how long it will take before Edward receives my letter.

Your devoted sister,
Athena Cranworth.

****

To Cliffton House

Middlethorpe

October 15th, 1805

Dearest Sister,

I could not help but write you again so soon for the house is all
in uproar this morning. Sir Simon was at our door as soon as was
decently possible and the breakfast things barely taken away. He
came to announce that Mrs Brindle has done 'him' the honour of
agreeing to be his wife to which Aunt replied rather coarsely,
"Well, Lachley, you've had the honeymoon you might as well
have the wedding." He was a little awkward with her at this
observation for he knows full well that he has brought his town
behaviour to Aunt's front door as well as his own. But that is not
all; the kitchen maid is expected to produce Sir Simon's only
[known] child any day now and he is determined to keep and
acknowledge it and would have Mrs Brindle accept it, for she is
childless also and that they should bring it up as their own.

By all accounts Mrs Brindle is beside herself and
overcome with joy at the prospect of becoming Lady Lachley,
genteel and a mama in a fraction of the time that it takes to
become worthy of such prizes but what other kind of woman
would take on a husband's by-blow so openly. However, Sir
Simon is not so blind to Mrs Brindle's short comings and would
not take her back to town as his wife until she is able to pretend
with any credibility that she is a lady and only coincidentally in
likeness to the landlady of The Olde Nag and has asked our great
aunt and myself to school her in all those gentilities that
otherwise take a lifetime to assimilate, for he would not engage
even the best tutors to come to The Larches lest they gossip upon
their return to London and bring all Mrs Brindle's necessary
efforts to nought and the facts of them printed in *The Morning
Post* and worse, become a matter for the coffee-house on-dit
supporters of the Whig, Charles James Fox*. Oh, how the
chickens return to the roost but if we are not to see her
condemned for the most vulgar of mushrooms, we must comply
with those wishes which the impudent man has assumed upon
us. It seems we are to untangle Mrs Brindle's vowels and teach

her to walk like a lady, for she is much inclined to stride as if she were escorting a foxed* customer from the premises or rolling a barrel. We are also to school her in the manner of dress. According to Aunt, and I would have you imagine now, Sister, that I whisper this to you in all confidentiality, Sir Simon requires us to teach her the rules of the sort of fashionable dress which never gives cause for comment from the most influential of society. No need for any reading between lines there I think, but it seems Sir Simon has a great partiality for her own very particular manner of dress but has told her that it must remain between them, that is to say, in the house only and not even before the servants and most decidedly not for public consumption. This will give you no little idea of the 'lady' herself and is a far better description of the bonfire outfit than any words I could choose and surely this is yet further evidence of Sir Simon's true preferences and I wonder at it that he would own any of it to our great aunt. We are not yet done; he would also have her taught to handle the Phaeton, as he believes her ability to do so will do much to convince that she is a lady though it is certain that even if we succeed with our charge, her origins will have to remain very obscure indeed. Aunt has, therefore, insisted that Mrs Brindle must be moved into Middlethorpe, not only for our convenience, for fear that if we are to achieve anything before the grave looms, school must begin early in the day and finish late at night but also as a first step in convincing society that she is not a 'barque of frailty'*, especially from amongst those who think to recognise her from The Olde Nag.

Do you know, Kate, I rather think that my resounding refusal of Sir Simon has actually served to bring him about; God redeems where humankind is not inclined. I believe we are about to see this degenerate creature cease his endless carousing and stay home with his legalised light 'o' love* and together raise the last of his side-slips*. I fancy my life has become far more interesting than your own dearest Kate, for I am inclined to think that brushing against the not quite respectable does possess a certain frisson.

Now I shall expect you to write back post-haste to tell me that I should be ashamed to think it. I know how horrified you are at my use of common cant but you have no need to worry, I would never dream of using it in company but you must own that my present experiences do suit its usage rather well and it is only for your eyes dearest Sister. I trust you do not show all my letters to Cliffton for I fear he would be most shocked and might even forbid you to read them and then who should I have of my own without you [and Edward who is still so notably absent in my life].

Your devoted sister,
Athena Cranworth.

P.S.
Mr T has just arrived this very minute bringing with him a microscope and I hear his voice echoing up from the hall suggesting to Aunt that we might gather insects and pond water to submit to its revelations. How absolutely thrilling; at last, I shall see the universe in a drop of teeming water and no doubt discover once and for all why we forbear to drink it.

****

To Middlethorpe

Blackthorn's Farm
Longburn
Northumberland

October 18th, 1805

Dear Miss Athena,

I would have wrote you sooner but had no way of knowing where you was. I knew you were sent to your Great Aunt Middlethorpe but had no idea of her whereabouts that is until John Maudent knocked on our door. There's been a lot gone on that shouldn't have, Miss Athena, and as far as I can see, all of it against you. I was sent away by your ma and pa on account as I can read and write and they was fearful as I would learn all, as servants do, and telling you of it after they sent you away.

It started when Miss Katherine came to stay with you and I know as she brought a letter with her which I know for a fact was showed to your parents but not to you and whatever was in it was kept from you. When they saw that I had seen this though I tried to pretend that I had not, your father told me that I must pack my bags and be gone and not to speak to you or to say farewell. He drove me into Hilling his self and booked me a seat to Morpeth and told me as I would need to get myself on either a stage or mail coach the rest of the way. But the coach from Hilling didn't leave until the morning and I was obliged to stay the night in the inn on my own. Your father has little thought for a girl of my class being unaccompanied in one of those places for we are fair sport to gentlemen and not alike, though he gave me enough money to pay for everything and to keep me going awhile after. My own ma and da was fair shocked to see me home and I had a mountain of convincing to do afore they would believe that I had not done something to offend and been given my marching orders. It's a sennight since John Maudent arrived at our door with a story. For a start, he could tell me where you were now put and what you was about, being sent to your ancient great aunt to companion and nurse her and you being deprived of your last chance at the Season. He said how you gave him the books and some money and a letter of praise and he was right upset by it all, Ma'am, and said how you had been cheated and treated ill.

Yet I know it for the truth that your parents were planning your Season and had no intention of depriving you of it until Miss Katherine as is Mrs Cliffton came and I know as she is behind it along with that letter because when I was packing up my belongings, I had to go in the domestic garden to get a dress of mine that were drying in the sun and it backs onto the rose garden being divided by a hedge. Begging your pardon, Miss Athena, I stood behind that hedge and listened to your parents and Miss Kate saying as you would never know the truth and that Master Edward must never be told neither as he would be on your side and as he would make your pa stump up the blunt* for another Season. Oh, Miss Athena, I went and sneezed, I always did sneeze in outdoor places as you know right well which is why I prefer to be indoors and I been sneezing nonstop since I got home but the point being, I was only a foot from them and they heard me and that meant they knew as I had heard them. They couldn't get me out of the house quick enough. Would I be right in guessing they have told you not to write to Master Edward for it seems likely if they don't want him to know what has happened to you?

Now, here's the bit as you won't want to hear, Miss Athena. Soon as they saw the books you gave John and your plans to write and teach him by correspondence well, that is to say, they knew he and me were friends and of his new great allegiance to you and they weren't going to take any chances that as soon as he could write a bit, he would let me know where you were to be found so they told him he had to leave so as you would not be able to teach him by letter. He made his way to London and did some work there but then decided to use the money you gave him to come and see me as he was afraid of what might become of him at the hands of your great aunt if he made his way back to you although he was terrible troubled by what had befallen you. I have been teaching him his letters and numbers as you would have wished, Miss Athena, and he learns quick and wants to add his few words to mine as he can manage.

DEAR MISS ATHENA, I HOPE YOO R NOT SAD WITH YORE ARNT. SOON I WILL RITE BETTER AND WEN I DO I WILL MAKE YOO PROWD AND NOT BE A LOW SERVENT ANY MORE.

MY RESPECT—JON.

He works day and night to learn, Miss, and helps my da on the farm for his keep. Would you be kind enough to write back and tell us what is happening to you and if Master Edward knows what has been done to you? I'm sure we will find the money to pay the post boy when it arrives. John still has some left of what you gave him.

My true affections,
From your devoted lady's maid,
Grace Blackthorn

****

To Mrs Katherine Cliffton   Middlethorpe
Cliffton House
Medford
West Suffolk

October 23rd, 1805

It is with the profoundest sadness that I have received a letter from my lady's maid, Grace Blackthorn with a contribution by John Maudent, both of whom, if their story is to be believed, have indeed been treated most heinously by our family. I have never known either servant to be anything other than scrupulously honest and therefore I must believe the worst.

It seems, Madam, you are behind a plot to ensure that I did not find a husband in what was generally assumed by all to be my final Season, for achieving that end which is expected of all females but though I rack my brain all night I cannot comprehend any reason for you to do this. I am given to understand that you arrived at Kestlehurst bearing a letter to which I was not made privy and I think therein lies the answer to this most pernicious of mysteries. I have spoken to Great Aunt Horatia and she is completely defeated as to rhyme or reason for this most unsisterly of plots. All she can tell me is that Papa requested that she take me as a companion for the remainder of her life, which being a Middlethorpe well past the milestone year of seventy and in radiant good health was like to mean that I would be here for many years to come and well out of the way of whatever plan you and the devil have hatched between you. He complained to her that my plain looks, bookish ways and unfeminine inclination to opinion had made him and Mama a laughing stock at every Season and that Almacks* had dealt the final blow to their dignity and my chances and would no longer issue vouchers to us, for I am considered an ill example of the wares they usually offer on the marriage mart and the advancement of my years in the unmarried state, proof of the same. I believe this to be an entire fabrication on Papa's part. My looks may not be of the best but many a bran-faced* creature may be found at the best places and my dowry at eight thousand pounds is not without enticement.

I am yet to hear from Edward but when I do, I have been given good reason to believe that he will have no knowledge of the embargo put upon receiving of letters from his family or only through official channels.

It now behoves you, Madam, to make a confession as to your part in this matter and to produce a credible reason for it. You may be assured that as soon as I have word from our brother, he will hear of this and I would, if it be possible, have him temporarily relieved of duty that he might return home and demand the truth of you all.

Thus far I am broken hearted but I feel that the grey cloud that hangs over me is yet filled with more tears to come. The story and its purpose is incomplete and I would have it all and know the full extent of my family's treachery and abandonment of me and I cannot, will not, believe that Edward is part of it. How comes it that the only people I can trust from beneath the roof of Kestlehurst are two servants who have been as vilified and as ill-used as I and have nothing to gain from their honourable stand.

No sister or daughter was ever more ill-used. If you are happy in your married state as I believe you to be, what possible reason could you have to deny me the same?

Athena Cranworth.

****

To Miss A. Cranworth
Middlethorpe
Loosmore
Hampshire

Cliffton House
Medford
West Suffolk

October 26th, 1805

Dear Madam,

I am charged by Mr and Mrs Charles Cliffton to inform you that they have departed with their children to visit a number of Mr Cliffton's family members who reside in various parts of the country. Intending to travel extensively they will therefore not be contactable at any reliable address. It has, therefore, been left to me to answer any letters as best I can. It has also been suggested that Mr Cliffton's desire to travel abroad might be undertaken in some small way after his visits to his relatives have been completed. If I can be of any further assistance, Ma'am, please do not hesitate to contact me.

I am yours respectfully,
Nathanial Bedlow: Secretary.

****

To Mr N. Bedlow: Secretary
Cliffton House
Medford

West Suffolk

Middlethorpe
Loosmore

Hampshire

October 29th, 1805

Dear Sir,

Be pleased to inform my craven sister and brother-in-law that I do not believe them to be other than at home, unless that is they have gone to ground at Kestlehurst for need of a safe house in which to hide their shame along with their fellows, those unblushing traitors to parenthood, for whatever it is they have attempted upon me.

The whole world knows that this is the time of year when the roads are about to become un-navigable. It is risky enough when one needs must go anywhere at this time of year, most particularly when undertaking one's Season but no one undertakes a grand tour expected to last as many months as makes winter. As to Mr Cliffton's desire to investigate foreign climes, may I please suggest that he avails himself of a newspaper from time to time and on the strength of their content in these troubled days would beg him to leave his children in this country as Bonaparte is everywhere at present and would be king of every inch of ground he bloodies. No, Sir, my sister and brother-in-law do not plan to go abroad and you and they must think me very dull of mind to believe it.

The fact that Mr Cliffton has apparently scuttled into hiding with his wife, my sister, proves to me that they have both become embroiled in something shameful in which he has been led by the nose and you, Sir, have been added to their shame for they would have you beggar the truth to one of their own.

How relieving it is to learn that not all our countrymen are as my own family or the ones that some of them marry into or employ for but eight days since, we learn that Admiral Lord Nelson is gone from us at The Battle of Trafalgar where he earned a decisive victory but at the cost of his most courageous and noble life.

Please be good enough to hand this letter to my errant sister and brother-in-law as soon as it arrives.

Yours respectfully,
Athena Cranworth.

****

To Baron Edward Cranworth von Wittenstein   Middlethorpe
The Royal Palace   Loosmore
Lower Wittenstein   Hampshire

November 10th, 1805

My Dearest Brother,

You cannot know how relieved I am to hear from you at last but your news is above and beyond tragic. How terribly consumed by sadness you must be dearest Edward and I wish with all my heart that I were with you to comfort you in your great distress but alas, instead I added to your grief with my own. How shocked I was to eventually learn of the great changes to your life which you have undergone and all knowledge of them denied me in the name of treachery. Be that as it may, I think you must have been right when you said that your beloved princess was lacking in maturity for the rigours of marriage and yet I did understand her father's need for her to undertake her duty when one considers the alternative that will descend upon them from the north, anon. I cannot bear to think that all through the unconscionably enforced changes to my own life that I have been undergoing, in all that time, you have married, become a royal consort and lost both your first child and your wife to the grave and I knew nothing of any of it. I think that none of this can bode well for the health of your Royal father-in-law and that it must hasten his own death. I collect that this will mean that the odious Rodolphe von Witten will seize the throne, that is, if the equally odious Bonaparte doesn't hear about it and seize it first for at the present time he is much too close to your back door for my peace of mind and I think that the British Diplomatic Office must surely be closed down soon but shall you return home or stay with your beleaguered father-in-law. You will have had the news from Trafalgar of course; despatches would have ridden through the night to get it to you though our wicked family would have me believe otherwise.

Now my most precious brother, I must broach what I would not but there it is, it must be faced by both of us. Reading of what you have told us and reading between Kate's empty lines, it would seem from your subsequent very long letter to me that an imbroglio of some magnitude has been perpetrated upon me specifically but upon you also, as you have been vastly misled. As I understand it, you were obliged to give up your heirdom to Kestlehurst. As the father of an heir to the throne of L W, the position would place many problems upon your shoulders. Through a Regency set up in the event of the Prince's illness rendering him incapable of carrying out his royal duty, thus protection of the Princess and the Kingdom and any legal heirs from the threat by R von W would be assured. Of course, the Prince saw it as absolute necessity that you should remain at all times within the perimeters of LW until such time as stability came to pass in the region which in truth did not look at all likely and even less so now. With these things in mind, you saw a parallel, if lesser, situation at Kestlehurst and as such it was my right and duty as the eldest to produce an heir for the estate and to that end all effort on our parents' part and mine should be undertaken. However, the letter explaining all this to our parents and me being destroyed, you relied upon our sister to send her version of the same letter to them and therefore me also.

Sadly, you must learn that our sister had other ideas and thought to have me driven out to permanent spinsterhood so that her own son Cyril would become the heir to Kestlehurst. I have to tell you, Edward, that if it had not been for two servants that were also cruelly driven out by our parents for what one half knew and the other was likely to learn, I would have been none the wiser to any of it until it was too late. You bid Kate tell me to make all effort against my natural plainness for this, possibly my last Season but she talked our parents around to denying me that, convincing Papa that it would be another vast sum of money, yet again spent to no result. She cared nothing that I would become that creature most despised by society, an 'old maid'. The letters you say that you sent to me at Kestlehurst must still be there or destroyed. I am sure that Quigley would have directed them to me had he been allowed to do so, he is always first on the scene when post arrives and he instantly directs it to whomsoever it is addressed. He may be the most ill-tempered butler that ever lived but he is assiduous in his sense of duty and would have considered it a matter of immediate import that your mail was got to me as quickly as possible. I suspect that either

Mama or Papa got to it first and to this day Quigley knows nothing of its existence.

I have been led to believe by Kate that Mama ails and badly so that I should have myself at the ready to return to Kestlehurst to do my duty towards her but a letter from Dr Carswell in reply to my own assures me that there must have been some error in the matter as he has not been called out to her these three years since and must assume that she goes on as remarkably well as most Middlethorpes and, therefore, I must judge that this monstrous lie was fabricated in the face of my new highly social position here at Middlethorpe to ensure that I remained unmarried and, therefore, childless. Have you ever heard such a tangled deceit? That our sister who has produced such beautiful children should have hatched such a stinking egg will ever remain a source of unbelief for me; only you dear Brother will be able to comprehend the unbearable pain I feel. Our great aunt and her friend Mrs Comfort have gathered about me in their attempts to buffer me against the arrows of familial treachery that continue to pierce my heart day and night. Such terms of endearment as I used in every letter I wrote to Kate that she would always be sensible of my enduring love of her; did they never prick her conscience, did they never cause her a moment's doubt upon her chosen course? I fear they did not and for that reason, I must leave her to make her peace with God alone for I shall not accompany her on that most formidable of journeys. You must know, Edward, that Mrs Winifred Comfort is the most prodigious of gossips and will omit nothing; this means that Sir Simon Lachley will have had it all already. Being a frequenter of the London coffee-houses and also a most shameless practitioner of 'on-dit' imaginable, the Clifftons' reputations will likely be in shreds as I write and Cliffton's career in question if it be known that he and his wife were ready to plunge the Brutus knife into the back of one of their own, a vulnerable spinster sister; will anyone ever entrust him again with their affairs of business. I fear they have set their own course of judgment and punishment at the hands of society by whom they both set so much store. Cliffton's weak-mindedness in the plot will encourage him to blame Kate for his share in their downfall and there will not be a moment's happiness in their marriage hereafter. Oh, Edward, think not that I relish it, no, not for one moment. Kate's shame will pain me as much as her and her daughters will need be sold to the highest bidder after all and what of poor little Baby Cyril now. I fear he will have nothing to inherit and I think that we must help him when the time comes.

I shall be delirious with joy when—or if I should learn of your intentions to return to England and assume your true role as heir to Kestlehurst. The very thought that the Clifftons would take it over in preparation for Cyril's majority fills me with anger and indignation for they deserve nothing less than opprobrium. The death of your lovely princess and infant has proved a great and even ironic punishment of them though it be the worst of tragedies upon you, my poor brother. I cannot believe that I feel so much vitriol towards a younger sister who I have loved so well and with all my soul. She was more beautiful than I, yet I felt no resentment of it. She had every beau of the Season at her heels, yet I rejoiced for her. Her abilities to dance and sing and flirt were everything I did not possess, yet I accepted with good heart what God had given her and not me. Instead, I treasured my own inclinations to learning and edging towards those liberties that the female is not expected to enjoy, such as opinion and rhetoric. These things, of course, have left me on the cold and draughty shelf to gather the dust of the advancing and unkind years, not to mention the unkindness of those better situated.

But away with all these grey clouds for I find myself most perfectly situated and contrary to all expectations am vastly happy. Great Aunt Middlethorpe shares my proclivities and owns a library to challenge that of any man of scholarship and my opinions and request for knowledge are tolerated by her friends if not approved of, save for one who enjoys to fulfil my needs in these matters for he is a Fellow of The Royal Society, Mr Marcus Temple, I think you should like him very well, Edward. He does not shun me nor hold a disgust of me, neither does he mock me for having a brain that is likely to overheat into hysteria if taxed by matters too far above what God supposedly designed me for.

Furthermore dearest Edward, I think you might approve my new look for I am very modern these days thanks to Great Aunt and my new lady's maid Mary but if it avails me anything I am thankful it will not be to take Kestlehurst away from you but, in truth, I am sure it will not for I am inclined to think that in spite of my unaccustomed pleasure when now looking in the mirror, I am sure my enduring plainness gets the better of even the highest fashion for it pokes through like a needle left behind in a beautiful gown.

As I write these words, Brother, I am assailed by a thought which has not hitherto occurred. Notwithstanding the Middlethorpe longevity and that Mama and Papa are not yet considered old, Papa is but one and fifty and in robust health and therefore, you are unlikely to inherit for some time. Please forgive this foray into selfishness on my part but what must happen to me between the deaths of Great Aunt Middlethorpe and that of our parents. Nothing could induce me to return home while our parents live and I have insufficient money of my own since I am unmarried. I am loath to add to your concerns when you have so many; it seems the grey clouds will have their way after all. My love and prayerful support follow you everywhere my dearest Edward.

Your devoted sister,
Athena Cranworth.

****

To Baron Edward Cranworth von Wittenstein Middlethorpe
The Royal Palace
Lower Wittenstein

November 30th, 1805

My Dearest Brother,

My deepest condolences on the recent loss of your father-in-law the Prince; indeed his lot was heavy in his last days and must have served to bring him to a swift and sudden end, for what did he have to live. You are right when you say there is nothing more you can do to serve them, they must have the setting up of their regency and you can now play no part in that. Your time amongst them has been too short and sadly lacking in success for you to claim that level of power or influence and now that the armies gather to beat back the ambitions of R von W of UW, it is better that you depart that country and the British Diplomatic Office be closed down before it becomes impossible for you all to leave, for from what I hear of the callow Rudolph von W, he is unlikely to acknowledge the observances and privileges of ambassadorial office and would throw you and the ambassador himself into prison for as long as it please him to do so.

What a fearful thing it is when mere boys of ill temperament have crowns and armies to play with. It would be the most wonderful seasonal gift if we could have you home for Christmas. I know Great Aunt would be delighted if you would choose to spend it here at Middlethorpe and I should very much like to introduce you to Mr Marcus Temple, I think you two would enjoy much stimulating conversation and of course all our other friends also, who are equally stimulating but for differing reasons. We recently had an autumn wedding—in every sense of the word for our local ageing roué, Sir Simon Lachley, married a similarly ageing Mrs Brindle of dubious origin but they are every bit smelling of April and May* as any young pair of lovers and now they parent a little baby boy who bears the unmistakable looks of the bridegroom but born to the scullery maid before the wedding. They have called him John rather than Simon for his father's reputation goes well before him as does his grandfather's and it was thought it might give the boy a sporting chance later in life if he were not to share their first name. I think it might have worked a great deal better had they forsworn the name of Lachley entirely for Brindle. I do hope you are not completely shocked by such shocking news and I beg you not think that I am fallen among degenerate company for we acknowledge all the demands of polite society but rather less of the hypocrisies. [That is Great Aunt's answer for it anyhow and I am inclined to repeat it.]

It is besides my determined wish that you spend some time here at Middlethorpe learning how Great Aunt runs her estate for it bears no comparison to the way in which Kestlehurst is governed and I would have you a better Master than our father who is ever held somewhere between fear and dislike. Our great aunt is loved and revered and with good reason. She has worked harder than any woman and most men I know of to make Middlethorpe the envy of all and she was much vilified for her intent, most especially by Mr Temple's grandfather who said much on the subject at the time of her widowhood against any possibility that a woman could run anything let alone a vast estate and that it would all come to a ruinous end. He pronounced that her infamous and unnatural stand against remarriage would remain the talk of the eighteenth century and thus it was, no doubt, ensured by the efforts of the old gentleman himself right up until she reached her fiftieth year when they all finally ceased their attacks upon her. Mr Temple grew up hearing this prophecy of woe at regular intervals, usually after a successful Middlethorpe harvest, which went much against the grain, [I thought this a fine joke as did Aunt], yet her promulgated failure was never fulfilled and he resolved at the age of ten years to make himself known to Aunt as soon as he came of age and could not be prevented from doing so, as he was much intrigued by her unfeminine abilities and they have been firm friends these nine years. She has now confessed to me that she is much concerned for the future of the estate as are the tenants. They know only too well that when Aunt dies, the estate will go into hands like our father's whether those hands be in the family or not and the storm clouds will swiftly gather over Middlethorpe as they do over so many estates.

There is a problem here akin to the one that has been forced upon the people of LW in that there is a distant cousin whose doting mama is keen to put forward for an heir to Middlethorpe.

He is known as The Hon. Darnley Middlethorpe [his first name is an indication of some distant relationship I believe but bad blood will out however long past]. It is understood that he is weak in character with a matching intellect and is, therefore, much given to something called blood and thunder* and the gaming tables and would no doubt, given half a chance find an ally in Sir Simon but not for long as the estate would sure to be forfeit to his habits. All this has played much on Aunt's mind of late and she has admitted to some regrets in marrying her husband, though she loved him as she could have loved no other and it was for this reason she has never remarried and, for this reason also, the battle to be free to run the estate, in truth, came second. He was her first cousin and the dead child she bore him, though he was himself dead before it was born was most cruelly deformed and could not have lived. She has since believed that first cousins should never marry for they are but brother and sister once removed and it must be wrong. I think that her life's work here at Middlethorpe has been atonement for it but I cannot see her as any kind of sinner but the best of women and more importantly, the best of people. She would not be the first to undertake such a marriage and the clergyman who married them not the first to avert his cognisance of such a match but they were so well-suited otherwise and upon his untimely death Middlethorpe passed to a most worthy inheritor; surely the Almighty was behind such an outcome and, therefore, no sin committed; or could it be a case of a wrong wiped afresh by conversion into good.

My dearest Edward, have your recent experiences along with my own perchance caused you to think upon the rearing of females, for they cannot be said to be nurtured. I am inclined to think that a weak and untutored mind bodes ill in all matters. Had your beloved Ursulinde been possessed of a real education and been taught to think and reason, do not you suppose that she might have overcome her natural fragility sufficiently to have survived her loss of your child for I am much of the belief that the mind affects the body for good or ill. So many females suffer endless ailments and vapours, it can't all be put down to tight stays but I can and do put it down to the endless bolt and padlocks we are constrained to endure upon all that we are capable of. I ask you to consider, brother; would you not feel ill if you were

116

taught that, 'if you know anything, be sure to hide it or suffer the disgust it will engender.'

Whilst I make every effort to comfort our great aunt in her own continued grief and mull endlessly and uselessly upon the tragedy that is our family, I await your dear self.

Please write and say you are coming home dearest, Edward, and safely so and we will deck the halls together for the holly here is already rich with berries and the ivy begs to be plucked.

Your devoted sister,
Athena Cranworth.

****

Blackthorn Farm   Middlethorpe
Longburn
Northumberland

December l0th, 1805

My Dear Gracie and John,

Trusting that you and your parents are in continued good health, I write to you both this time with much-improved tidings. You will be delighted to hear that Mrs Cliffton's plotting has come to nought for Master Edward comes home and comes home for good. My last letter to him begging him to return was only left me some hours when I received yet further news from him. The heir to Kestlehurst will be back in his rightful place but first, he comes to see you. I have arranged for a special messenger from the Loosmore Mail Office carrying official documents to ride day and night if necessary to divert my letter which was of course sent to Wittenstein, to be delivered to Blackthorn Farm instead for he must know its contents. I have paid over a considerable sum for this service and you will not be required to hand over any monies to the rider but I think he might be grateful for some rest and any refreshments you can provide and a few pennies for himself for it is a hard ride that he undertakes.

You may be assured that my brother will reimburse you; he travels across land at an awkward angle to avoid the Borders of Upper Wittenstein where he could encounter difficulties and thence to the north of Denmark where he will set sail for Newcastle. I know not when he will arrive as the journey is surely long and arduous but it is certain that he is well upon his way as I write and you should expect him soon. You are not to vex yourselves over the matter of lodgings; he will stay at a coaching inn at Morpeth for the night. Now to the reason for this visit; my brother will leave monies with you that will enable you to accept letters from me and to facilitate your coming into Hampshire for it is my intent that you shall both have work here at Middlethorpe if you are so inclined. I intend John for training up to my secretary for I shall have need of one and I know that once he is sufficiently educated, he will be the most trusted of servants and will be able to boast a situation of some import. As to you, my dear Gracie, whom I have missed much, you will return as my lady's maid. Mary, who has been an inspiration in my recent modernisation, is to marry a tenant farmer, one Joseph Pennyweather who has recently taken over from his father having lately suffered an apoplexy* that has left him bedridden. Joseph's mother will have a great burden in looking after him and it is therefore of some urgency that Joseph marry and as he and Mary have been sweethearts since childhood, it is right that they should wed which they will do at Christmas. As to me and my need for a secretary though at a later date, well, I have news that may come as a surprise.

I have lately become much acquainted with a gentleman of whom I have spoken and I know that we have both been victims of Great Aunt Middlethorpe's conniving for she brought to her table the sort of young females that Mr Marcus Temple thought himself in need of cultivating. Though not entirely penniless, there is little to show for his existence as he is a victim of primogeniture. As is perfectly usual, he looked for an heiress but found them so completely vacant to his own calling as to be the stuff of gothic nightmares and the thought of spending long evenings in the company of a wife whose only training was in flirting her way into a suitable marriage, and thereafter simpering her way through it that her lord and master should always know his own superiority in the match, was for Mr Temple beyond all endurance.

As you know, Gracie, I have always been inclined to learning and learning of a particular kind which requires long hours of study. How many times have you remonstrated with me over my preferences and how they sent all the beaux of The Season scuttling for rescue to some lily-brained, limp-limbed goose who would make them feel 'quite the thing'. Oh, how you scolded me, Gracie, when I failed to remember that I was supposed to be weak minded and helpless in the face of life. Well, let me tell you and I positively rejoice in repeating myself to anyone who was not present at the time and who is certain to be shocked that I even went as far as to say that I thought, only a stupid man could be in want of a stupid woman, moreover I said it at dinner, before all; what say you to that. Are you not shocked to despair of my incautious courage? As you may well imagine it caused all manner of stir about the dining table but though I had no idea of it at the time, the remark set my course for the future and set it fair, for Mr Marcus Temple has asked me to be his wife and we are to be married in that most traditional month of May. I am all happiness and I am resolved upon it, Gracie, you shall be a bridesmaid to me whatever society may think to it. However, I'm afraid I must give way to boasting and tell you that his offer for me was only the second since I have come to Middlethorpe but as to the first I will save the details until your arrival, for the gentleman concerned has been the subject of wild gossip all his life and is since married to another; if I keep the details of this scapegrace* secret until you come, it will give you something to look forward to, Gracie dear, and we shall be as merry together as we ever were.

Can I not say in all truth that life has held more excitement for me since my sister tried to destroy it than it ever did while she pretended to love me and for this reason I will forgive her— eventually, but am in no hurry to do so for there is no reason upon this earth why she and her wickedly-led husband should climb out of their mire so easily. I believe I should leave them both to it and give them the opportunity to approach me for forgiveness with at least a semblance of humility and one could hope sorrow. I do not wish to make an opera of it, you of all people know that I am not one to feed on sins or hurts that may have been done me but there is a limit to how much one should let others escape with, even if they are one's own sister or sadly, parents for that which is quickly or easily forgiven is soon forgotten by the perpetrators and they lose all awareness of the harm they have done and the pain they have caused.

And now I come to the very last piece of gold at the foot of my rainbow. Great Aunt has made me the heir to Middlethorpe. When Papa wrote informing her of my ill-favoured looks which he put down to my unfeminine tendencies to learning and his need to be rid of me thereby in the minds of others eventually being forgotten as the 'ape leader'* of the Cranworths who failed to make a match, she thought him in serious want of fatherly love and resolved that I deserved better and that given my ability for intelligent thought and being a Middlethorpe through Mama, I might be the very one to take on the mantle of the estate. As to my looks, she should see for herself if what Papa spoke was true or so much fudge* and fustion* but even if it be true, she is not so outmoded in her own reasoning as to believe it to have ought to do with the reading of books. Of course, she could not know then that his desire to be rid of me was in truth a need to have me out of the way before theirs and my sister's plan could become obvious to me. It occurs to me as I write that the greatest sadness of this wicked trickery is that if Papa and Kate had come to me in all straight dealing honesty and asked me to move over for Kate's son, I would in all humility have seen the sense of it and obliged them in the matter.

As it is, the Middlethorpe tenants are all delight and entirely relieved to learn who their next mistress will be. When the time comes, Mr Temple will support me in the business of running the estate but continue his true work in the field of the sciences and I shall support him likewise. In this way I think we shall be great friends which I have sadly observed not to be the case in most marriages and so the fires that might be lit at the beginning of an alliance are soon gone out and nothing to kindle remains. As you have probably deduced, neither of us has fallen hopelessly into the other's arms but I have hopes that the condition of 'April and May' will come soon for I cannot see myself ever being happy or content with another; in truth, I think God put me aside until I could be brought by whatever means to Mr Temple's side.

I hope with all my heart that Great Aunt Horatia Middlethorpe lives for as many years as her Middlethorpe constitution will allow, I wish it that we might enjoy her for some years to come so that I might lavish care upon her when her frailty finally arrives.

I trust Marcus and I will be given the time to raise the family I never thought to have and make them fit to inherit before my own heavy responsibility sets upon my shoulders. By the time I and my husband must step up and take over, John will be well-fitted to be our secretary and man of business. You, John will be trained by all of us including Aunt's secretary Mr Quentin Pomphrey who has been with her above forty years. His ways may be quaint in the extreme and he may dress like a court cockscomb but there is nothing he does not know about running Middlethorpe, though Aunt pretends that he knows nothing and he pretends she is right and you will be busier than you can ever imagine. Your time helping on the Blackthorn's farm will have taught you a good deal of what it takes to understand tenant farmers. Their troubles are no less than those who own their farms and I know you will make a reeve of sensibility.

I wish us all a very Merry Christmas and the joys of the New Year affect us all in equal measure.

Your mistress and true friend,
Athena Cranworth.

****

Glossary

****

Almacks – Exclusive London venue of The Ton* where the marriageable of society could meet and requiring highly prized vouchers to gain entry.

Altitudes – Drunk.

Ape leader – Old maid; beyond marriageable age. From old proverb stating that failure to produce children dooms the female to lead apes in hell.

Apoplexy – Stroke.

Banbury story/tales – Cock and Bull stories.

Barque of frailty – Female of easy virtue.

Blood and thunder – A mixture of Port and Brandy.

Bluestocking – Female whose interests lie in intellectual conversation. Usually wore blue stockings to denote her leanings.

Bracket faced tabby – Ugly female, hard featured.

Bran-faced – Freckled.

Blunt – Money.

By blow – An illegitimate child.

Charles James Fox – Leader of the opposition to Prime Minister William Pitt

Consols – Consolidated annuities.

Duns – Debt, persistent creditor

Fichu – Lace or muslin modesty neck covering tucked into top of gown

Foxed – Intoxicated.

Fudge – Nonsense.

Fustion – Nonsense or pomposity.

Flight/fly up to the boughs – Fly off the handle, loss of temper, fly into a passion.

Hartshorn – Remedy given for nervous vapours & sometimes headache.

High in the instep – Haughty, an excess of pride, arrogance.

Hungary Water – Headache remedy.

India bonds – East India Company (trading).

Knocked-up – Exhausted.

Leg-shackled – Married.

Light 'o' love – A mistress.

Lightskirt/s – Prostitute/s

Living under the hatches – In debt.

Man milliner – Suggestive of gay or transvestite.

Mantua maker – Dress Maker.

Molly House – An establishment for male prostitution and a meeting house for gay males.

Morbid throat – Whooping cough.

Nightrail – Nightshirt, nightdress

Not a feather to fly with – Completely broke, no money.

On-dit – Gossip, (one says)

Passé – Outdated, old-fashioned.

Phaeton – Fancy carriage

Pitt (Mr William) The Younger – Prime Minister of the day. Elder died 1805.

Press – Large piece of furniture, often floor to ceiling, carrying heavy shelves in which garments and household linens were placed to press out the creases and to store.

Primogeniture – System whereby eldest male inherits entire estate for the sake of its preservation.

Rattle – One who talks too much.

Receipts – Old form of recipe.

Reticule – Handbag.

Rum or Rum'un – Strange odd or peculiar person.

Sarcenet, Sarcnet – A soft, silky fine woven fabric with hint of lustre.

Scapegrace – Someone beyond the moral pale.

Sennight – Seven days, old form for one week.

Side-slips – Illegitimate children.

Third Dance Rule – A couple dancing together for the third time at the same entertainment will be presumed to be announcing an engagement and if not gossip will ensue.

The Ton – Top level of society run by patronesses, see Almacks.

Top-Heavy – Drunk.

Vauxhall Gardens – Original theme park of all entertainments both good and ill, in Lambeth, London.

Vulgar mushroom – New rich, pushy and pretentious. Like fungus that comes up overnight.

Wet goose – Stupidity or simple mindedness.

With gratitude to *Georgette Heyer's Regency World* by Jennifer Kloester for many of the words and phrases included in this glossary.

****

****

****

****

*****

***

**

Future Titles

The Thorn in the Bower (2016) being my second book in the Austen style is conventionally written and a tale of love, change, rebirth and acceptance, with a nod to the early efforts of the bravest females to change the lot of their sisters against all that the society of the day would permit them. The only child of late breeding parents of considerable wealth, Miss Briar-Rose Bower is brought up and educated as if she had been a boy by her father, who is determined that upon his death, his great estate shall not leave for the lesser and incompetent hands of his or his wife's family. The decision is momentous at every level and travels through society's chain of gossip known as the on-dit. Enter an earl of less than noble intent who was once met by Sir William Bower when a child, the mysterious revelation that they are linked by old blood and a wretched tale of ignorance and its attendant cruelty that reveals itself through an anomaly in the daughter of Bower's eyes changes him forever. An adventure ensues through the means of the Season and Miss Bower's extreme education leads her into a deal of trouble in which her reputation is called into question by almost everyone and even compromised by one of the nobility's most infamous rakehells. Again, there is a good chortle to be had from characters that seem to be entirely of their own time but can still be recognised amongst us today.

The third book in the series is **Daughters of Gentlemen** (2017). This story takes us to the middling strata of Regency society from Cheshire to Dorset via the house of a rural physician who is a gentleman in everything but his purse. A widower with three daughters and three devoted and underpaid servants has a constant struggle to support and maintain his household in a backwater of needy farm folk, precariously balancing out his income against the wealthier folk of the town who are ever reluctant to pay their bills. A dutiful daughter of twenty-two who accompanies her father into territory considered unfitting for any female wishing to be regarded as respectable, a vastly troublesome teenager of fourteen and a delightful child of nine who prefers to spend her days up trees yet speaks with a sagacity far beyond her years makes for a house with all the amusement it can cope with. A vile character in the form of Miss Emerald Plumb, the town tabby of once noble birth, is the protagonist from hell that brings the best out in everyone else. Yet a further female enters the equation early in the story, bringing with her revelations of an uncomfortable nature but both charms and disturbs the physician's household in unexpected ways. A gardener-cum-general man in possession of 'the knowings' (there is one in every rural backwater), a housekeeper from the orphanage who could cook for royalty if she but knew it and a general maid who falls helplessly in love with a human god so far above her who also finds himself as the unlikely guest in the physician's house makes up the main cast of characters and is a study in how those brought up high with a sense of entitlement and expectation of deference to their position compared to those brought up for the world of thoughtfulness and duty make a mockery of society's reckoning of who is really the gentleman but above all, it is a tale of love and kindness and the lost art of respect shown, even when undeserved. There are no diamonds to be found in Larks Knoll, only the pearl of profound happiness discovered in satisfying exhaustion being the wages of a hard day's work and duty carried out without bitterness, or the profit motive—a somewhat despised concept these days.

My next title will be **The Ripened Fruit in the Orchard (2018),** the heir to an earldom and in service to the rake of the realm, the Prince Regent (George) is on a dual duty visit to a small town on his way to The Royal Pavilion in Brighton. On a mission for ostrich feathers of a most particular colour for his mother in the draper's establishment, he meets with a young woman who, he discovers to his amazement, shares part of his unusual family name. He cannot help but notice that her beauty is quite divinely ordered, although he has no interest in her for himself, being only the daughter of a deceased vicar and even he may not make a plaything of a female brought up as delicately as his own and in the inconvenient shadow of the church; that is if he is not be held for a blackguard to the condemnation of his family's name. However, when he learns from his father that there is all likelihood of her being a distant cousin, he hatches an unholy plan to ingratiate himself with her family—and thus affect her introduction as his personal gift to His Royal Highness. Her family would not dare to complain against the heir to the throne and swearing all innocence in the matter, his own name would remain clean of any scandal that might ensue and thus having a relative ensconced in the royal bed, his own ambitions within the palace assured. He does not bargain for the impudent interference of his secretary who is determined to save this girl, whoever she might be, from a truly ruinous scheme that was bound to destroy not just her, but her entire family and without a shadow of a doubt, his own career.